AYDEN

House of Frazier Book 3

KATHI S. BARTON

This is a work of fiction. Names, characters, places, and incidents are products of the author's imagination or are used fictitiously and are not to be construed as real. Any resemblance to actual events, locations, organizations, or persons, living or dead, is entirely coincidental.

World Castle Publishing, LLC
Pensacola, Florida

Prologue

Edmond was happy for the time that he got to spend with his brothers. But he also wanted to go back home, find Mac, and take her back to bed. They'd had so much fun. It was not funny fun, but it was seriously good fun over the last few days, and he couldn't help but find himself singing. He tried very hard not to do it around his brothers.

"You're being foolish again. And if you don't wipe that sappy smile off your face, I'm going to beat you until you're nothing left but a pile of fur." Edmond looked at his brother, Ayden, but didn't ask what was on his mind. "Just don't. All right? I don't want to hear how you're in so much love that you can't leave the house and that spending time with us isn't working out for you."

"What's up your ass? He's here, isn't he?" It wasn't him who asked, but he was glad that Ivan had. "You've been picking and bitching since I picked you up. Tell us, or I'm really going to beat you until you're not even good enough for a pillow."

"Where is Lica? Tell me that." Edmond thought that there was more going on than him just being a prick right now. "When Brandy calls, we all jump to her bidding. Well, I've decided that I'm going to walk to my own drummer. You fuckers can do what she wants, but I'm going to branch out on my own and make my own cash."

"If you don't tell me what's wrong with you, I'm going to tell Brandy what you said. And you'll make her cry. Again. She's breeding, and you've made her cry three times in the last week. I don't know how much more that Lica can take of you doing that, but I'm willing to just skip over the part where you explain and beat the shit out of you because I can." Guy stood up and towered over Ayden. "Spill it, or I'm going to spill you all over this nice clean floor."

"I don't fucking want to meet my mate. All right? Look at him. He's sitting there wishing that he was anywhere but with me. Us." Everyone turned to look at him, and he shrugged. "Don't give me that shit. I saw the way you looked at Mac when she dropped you off. You'd rather be with her."

"You're making it so that none of us want to be with you. What the fuck, Ayden? Do you need a vacation? Lica said that you were working yourself too hard." Ayden asked him why they were talking about him. "Because, shithead, we're worried about you. I'm seriously thinking of taking you to see a head doctor to see if you've gotten a knot in your noodle. Tell us, or I'm going to leave. I don't need this kind of shit going on when I just want to chill out and spend some time with you guys. Do you remember why Lica isn't here? This is the day that Brandy has her ultrasound. He told us that last week and the week before how he wasn't going to miss that and wanted us to change—you're the one who told him it would be fine. That he'd better be bringing us back some pictures of the little guy."

"I forgot." They all snorted at Ayden, and then he looked around the table. Edmond thought that there was still more to whatever was up his ass and was, like the others, just grateful to be with his brothers. "What do you have to say for yourself? Mac going to be carting your ass around all the time too?" He'd been wrong in thinking that Ayden was in a better mood now.

"No." He had to count to ten twice before he trusted himself to speak. "I also told you that she was going to go and pick up her new car today. Since mine was here first, she's going to go there, and one of the drivers on the lot is going to bring my car back here. So that I could be here with you, whiney ass."

Ayden stood up so quickly that he felt his wolf race over his skin. He could feel him there as if he was ready for whatever his brother did. Edmond stood up, too, slower, and put both his hands up to make sure that Ayden didn't try to hurt him. He knew that in the mood he was in right now, he would tear him apart. Not kill him, but to hurt him badly.

"Sit down and cool the fuck off before I toss the lot of you out of here on your fucking ears. You're scaring the kids here. And you're not doing so good with my fear either. Sit the fuck down." Ayden sat down. Hard, like the woman standing there, he didn't know her name had a bit of alpha in her. "Now, order or don't, but you're not going to take up my best table with your bickering like five-year-olds. I have two at home right now, and I believe they have better manners than you do."

They each mumbled that they were sorry, and she didn't seem to like that either. Smacking the back of Ayden's head, he really was the cause of all this. She pointed her pen at them as she dressed them down. Christ, he wondered if Brandy or Mac had taken lessons from her.

"Now, this is the way it's going to be. You're going to order something to eat before I drag you out of here, and you're going to eat it, every morsel. I don't care if you have to puke it down in the bathroom but I don't want to have to buss this table only to find out that you've made a mess under the table as well." She hit Ayden again. "You're lucky to have family here with you, moron. You have been bitching a great deal. Now order. And so help me, if you don't leave me a reasonable tip, I'm going to hunt each of you down and make you eat it. Are we clear on that?"

They each gave her their order, and she took it, even going so far as to ask them questions that would need to be asked, like what sort of dressing did they want. Was there something that they wanted on the side? By the time she walked away, they were all sitting up a little straighter and making sure that they were as polite as they could be. She was fucking scary.

When she brought their drinks, each of them helped her steady the tray that looked as heavy as she was. She told them her name was Summer and that she was sorry for busting their chops. Instead of them telling her that it was all right, Ayden stood up. None of them moved when he told her how sorry he was and put money in her apron. That seemed to have pissed her off more than them bitching.

"I don't want your money, dipshit. I didn't do anything to deserve it. Just sit down and tip me at the end like you're supposed to." She shoved the money, which looked like a hundred-dollar bill, into Ayden's shirt pocket before she left them again.

No one said anything for several minutes. Edmond thought that they were waiting on Ayden. He was older than his other brothers by about a year, but he didn't want to set him off again. Waiting for him to raise his head seemed impossibly long, but when he did, he had tears in his eyes.

"I'm so sorry." None of them told him that it was all right. It wasn't, but he was their brother, and they'd do anything for any one of them. He knew that he would. "I've been house hunting like the rest of you were, and I was hit on with every person that, Christ, guys, men were hitting on me. I don't have a problem with how they hang, but he'd embarrassed me so badly that I left the house I was looking at for fear of what he'd do to me. It's the money. They don't want us. They want what they think we have being related to Brandy."

"Gee, thanks." Everyone laughed at him but for Ayden. "Look, I know what you mean. It's like…I told you guys about Mac's grandma, didn't I? All she cares about is how much she can get out of Mac and me before she keels over. That's in her mind, too. That we're going to somehow have this amazing bank account with a lot of zeros in it and that's going to be their ticket. To what? I have no idea, but it's out there, and I'm afraid of it. I think that from now on, we go in packs to look around. I'll be willing to lend you Mac, too. You know that she'll not put up with anything. She told me the other day that she only tolerates me so that she can have normal brothers. She actually thinks that you guys are normal. I have no idea where she gets that information, but there you have it."

"The other day, I was met at my office with my cleaning lady's daughter, naked, guys. She was standing there like she had better things to do than to hang out with me, but she was willing to do all the stuff I wanted. Stuff? Christ, that was scary as fuck." Guy looked around the room and told them that they should watch their language with the kids being around. They all agreed, and Guy continued. "I had to call the police to get her out of my office. Of course, I was so taken aback that I couldn't look them in the face. Or I don't know, they were embarrassed for me. But I don't want that kind of life either."

By the time their food came, they were all in a much better mood. Especially Ayden. He'd had a rough time of it lately. In working with Brandy, being her undercover man, so to speak, he'd been at a restaurant that had been—even to think about it made him a little ill—they were serving human meat instead of the things that were being bought for the restaurant, which they were selling off for more cash. Ayden hadn't been able to eat anything that might bleed onto his plate, and red meat was out of the question. Edmond didn't blame him one bit for that, either.

The rest of them, including him worked for Brandy and Lica too. A couple of days ago he'd been sent some paperwork on nine buildings in the next town over. He was to go there and inspect them. For wall standability. If they had electric as well as what the voltage that it could take. He'd never known that there was so much that a person had to look at to simply purchase a building. It had made him a little more aware of the buildings that he went into as well, like the one that were sitting in now. There was so much going on with it that he would have recommended tearing it down. But he loved the old place. It had a lot of good memories for him.

After their food mess was taken away, he sat with his brothers until Lica came in with Brandy. She was getting so big—not that he'd say that to her. But she seemed to shine with her new status as being a mom soon. When she told them that she was leaving, they all moved over for her to be with them as they went over the pictures.

"He's a boy, just as Mac told me. I'm so excited." She pointed out things in the pictures that he wouldn't have been able to tell you what they were. But she was excited, and it made them feel so as well. When Summer came back, she asked if she could see the pictures too and was excited with them. "I've got a bit to go yet. But you can't believe how excited I am right now."

"I have two to eight year olds at home with my husband. Every day, I look at them and think to myself, I made that. I have trouble wrapping my head around that at times, too." Summer handed the pictures back to Brandy and smiled at the table. "I'm glad to see that the five of you have gotten your crap together. I'm sorry for yelling at you before, but you were making a huge ruckus when there was no need for it."

As they left, he had to laugh a little to himself when he noticed that they hadn't stiffed her at all on the tip. There were at least five hundred dollars there as well as a couple of twenties. It made him feel good that he was a part of a great family.

Once he was outside, he turned to face the sun and let it warm him to his bones. It was chilly out. They'd been remarking on that for days now. The trees were nearly all turned now. The sound of them crunching under his feet made him happy. Also, for the first time in their lives, they were going to have a big family holiday. Thanksgiving and Christmas were holidays that he'd never looked forward to before. However, this year? He was about as excited as he'd ever been.

"What are your plans for the day?" He smiled at Ayden and told him that he was free if he was. "I am. I want to make it up to you, too, for making fun of you being in love. I'm jealous, I think. That you have something so wonderful, more than I could hope for in a mate, and I'm sitting on the sidelines just waiting for it to happen to me." He looked hurt before turning away.

"What is it? Tell me so that I can help you out of the jam or whatever it is that you need for me to do." He told him it was nothing and started away. The two of them were still standing in front of the little diner as they spoke. "It is something. Tell me before I have to wrap you up in my web and figure it out on my own. It would be a good deal less funny to me if you were just to tell me."

"All right. When that woman, Summer, came to the table and yelled at us, all I could think about was having her in my bed. Not very smart of my first thought about her, but that's what I wanted. Then she said she had two kids at home. Again, my heart was singing when I realized I actually knew that I was not going to be a good dad to them. But she has a husband." It took him all of three seconds to realize what his brother was saying. He asked him if what he thought was true. "Yes. But she's also married with those two children. And I know that I can go in there, kill off her husband so that I can be there for her. Seems to take away from the fact that we're mates. Don't you think?"

"Then we'll ask her if she's happy." Ayden just stared at him. "All right. As soon as I said it, I knew that it was wrong. But there is something that we're missing here. Maybe they really aren't happy."

"Stop it, goof. She's married and therefore—" Edmond turned to see what his brother was looking at. It was Summer.

"Did either one of you idiots drive here?" Ayden said that he did. "Good. Please, I need for you to—" She let out several calming breaths. It didn't seem to make her any less intense, but he wanted to help her as she struggled with it. "I need a ride to my house. I've already called the police so I would like to...I need to get there before the police. They won't allow me in if they're there first."

"Your husband or your children?" She didn't voice her answer but did nod at him. As they made their way to the parking lot, she didn't seem to mind him going along, so Edmond got into the back seat. Whatever was going on, he was going to be there for his brother.

"I need for you all to meet me at Fourteen Zero Seven, Chestnut Street. I don't know what's going on, but something has our waitress stressed out." He put his hand on his brother's shoulder and gave it a tight squeeze. The other brothers, including Mac and Brandy, said that they were on their way. *"Good. Thank you. The police are on their way, so if one of you could go in and check on the husband and children, again, I don't know what's going on, I'll be ever so grateful."*

Each of them said that they were on their way again. Ayden was asking Summer questions about whether she knew what was going on or if someone had called her. Anything to get information without shaking her. He could tell that Ayden wanted to shake the need out of her, but he was talking to her as calmly as he supposed that he could.

"My neighbor called telling me that there was screaming coming from my place. She didn't know if it was the girls or not playing in the backyard. She just wanted them to stop." Summer was soft but continued. "She actually has asked me not to let the herd, my children, out when she's trying to have a card party. Stupid woman. Doesn't she understand that, firstly, they're not cows, so there is no herd. Secondly, they're playing as children do."

"What made it different this time for her to call you?" Summer looked at him like she'd never seen him before. "It's all right if you don't know. We'll be there for you anyway."

"Selma, Selma and Harley, short for Harlequin, said that they didn't want to stay with their dad today. That the last time he was watching them, he'd not fed them, nor had he let them out of their room. I thought that I could trust him." She looked out the window of the car as they drove by several houses on her street. "That's a lie. I was desperate, and I needed to work. So I called and asked him, and he said he'd do that. But I had to pay him. Pay him? Like they're not his children as well."

As soon as they pulled into the driveway, Summer was out and running to the house. It was Brandy that caught her, telling her that she couldn't go in and that it was going to be a police crime scene. The harder she fought with Brandy, the more Brandy was determined not to allow her in.

"My daughters are in there, you fucking bitch. Let me pass." Brandy told Summer that the girls were fine, but she'd told them not to move. "What do you mean, not to move? If they're fine, then they need to come out here and come to me. Where is their father? Gilbert? Where is he?"

"Dead."

~*~

Mac kept an eye on Summer. Mac had only been back for about half an hour when the all-help message had hit her. Running to the house, their house closer than anyone else's, she was there in time to see that the little ones were all right, but Gilbert was dying. He'd not yet taken his last breath.

"Are you sure that they're all right?" She told the woman, for about the fifth time that they were, that no one would harm them while she was there. "That other woman, she told me that Gilbert was dead. How does she know that? I'd very much like to beat her right now, but I don't think it would do any of us any good."

"I know how you feel. She makes me want to punch her in her face several times a day." That was untrue, but it made Summer smile a little. "When I got here, I only live about two houses down from here on the next street over. He was still alive. It was doubtful to me that he'd had long to go, but I asked him who had killed him. The little girls, who are a great deal calmer than their mom is right now, told me what happened. I can tell you what they said to me, but the police asked me not to. Until they can talk to the girls."

"No, don't. I think that it would tear me apart to know that they had seen him killed. I also have a feeling that it had a great deal to do with the way he lives when not at the house. He's my ex-husband, by the way. I only tell men that we're married because it keeps other men from hitting on me. Not that anyone would want to take on a mentally unstable mom of two because of the things that Gilbert did to the three of us."

"Harley is the calmest. She's the one that

spoke to me. Selma was there as well, standing in the living room with her sister. They're beautiful, by the way." Summer thanked her. "Is that enough for now, or are you going to need more to be this calm?"

"I don't know, to be honest." When Summer looked around, so did Mac. "That man there, the one that you told me was your husband, is he all right? Today, when they were all in the restaurant, he seemed a bit on edge. I might have taken my bad mood out on the five of them."

"He's all right now. I think that he'd like to come over and sit with you. I know that it would calm you both down." She only nodded, and she asked Ayden to come and be with Summer. "I'm going to check on things for you both. As soon as I know anything, I'll let you guys know. But I swear on my love for Edmond, your children are perfectly fine."

The police were waiting for the coroner's office to come and get what they could from the crime scene. Mac, along with Edmond, knew what had happened in the house. The moment that she walked through the door, everything, even to the smallest detail, was there for her to see. Edmond too.

Gilbert had been sitting on the couch having a nap, and the girls were locked into their bedroom. Not on his side but on their own. That was going to take some explaining to Summer when she was able to see them. Why would they have their father locked out of their rooms? Since she'd never touched the girls, she couldn't tell yet. But she did know what had happened to Gilbert.

There were three men in the living room when shots were fired. The men were there to talk to Gilbert about his recent dips into their territory. Selling drugs in someone else's established market was a big no-no, she knew. But he was doing more than that, and the men were there to talk to him about it.

Gilbert was running drugs through Summer's house, using a post office box that he'd set up as her place to get mail as a drop point. Also, he would run his stable of women for prostitution while using his ex-wife's computer. Summer was unaware of it, but her daughters knew.

The girls were afraid to tell their mom for fear of their father. He'd threatened them with certain death and worse yet to sell them off to the highest bidder. Mac had a feeling that he'd do it too. The man was forever out for himself and didn't give a shit about the two little ones that used to depend on him when they were little. Not anymore. Not for a long time, either.

Officer Capshaw came to find her when she was standing at the door waiting for him. He only shook his head when he came out of the house. Behind him, she could see the little girls. They were being helped by a female officer out of their clothing and into a scrub shirt that was way too large for them.

As soon as they were dressed, they ran out of the house to their mom. Mac felt their love all the way across the yard to where she was standing. She looked at Capshaw when he cleared his throat.

"I'm not even going to ask you how you knew to look for the other men. You were right. They're all dead. Gilbert got off a few shots of his own. I will have nightmares for the rest of my life when I think about how close those bullets going through the door got to those little ones." He eyed her with a frown on his face. "How did you know that this was going on in the first place?"

She told him that Ayden and Edmond were

at the restaurant when Summer needed help. He nodded and then asked about the girls. Shaking her head, she told him she wasn't sure what he was talking about.

"I'm sure you do, but I'm going to leave that alone. For now. So long as nothing comes back to bite me in the balls about it." She assured him, like assuring the mom, told him that he was not going to be bitten by any of it. "Gilbert has a list of crimes that are longer than I am standing up. I guess the Feds were looking for him about a month ago, and he sort of skipped around until they left him here. I'm not saying that there would be fewer deaths had they really looked. There are three men off the lists of most wanted right now, and I'm happy with the results."

"I think that a great many people will be." He nodded and watched with her the reunion between a mother and her kids. "She's Ayden's mate. Or his? I'm not sure how they say that. The girls couldn't be any safer so long as he had breath in his body. Not to mention, they'll grow up not to be so terrified of every little thing. You know all of us well enough that we'll keep the three of them safe as well."

"You keep saying that. Like you know there is going to be trouble. Do you?" She told him that she didn't, not anymore. "I'm not sure what that means either, but I'm too overwhelmed right now to chase you down about it. Just tell me when something like this is going to happen, and I'll be as happy as I've ever been."

After talking, she made her way to Edmond. He was standing guard over the little family, and she was glad that someone was. Once one of the officers came to talk to Ayden and Summer, Edmond followed her to the furthest away car.

"It's all gone." She nodded at him, and he smiled at her. "I have to tell you, I'm sort of sad about that. It was neat knowing that I could use my green spider shit and wrap people up. It was like it was there for us to use just one time, and then it just faded away. I even asked Lica about the stuff we shared with him. He didn't know what I was talking about. Is that the way it was supposed to work, you think?"

"Yeah, I do." Mac looked up at the man of her dreams. "You know what happened in there, don't you? What I had to do?" He nodded and kissed her on the mouth.

"How do you feel about being able to save a life the way that I had. There were shots fired directly at the officer that day, right into his head. Had I not been there to wrap him up in that vine stuff, he would have surely died. The same way with Harlequin, too, I'm guessing."

She smiled at him when he asked her if she'd killed Gilbert. "Yes. He was holding his daughter hostage when I arrived. The bad guys had already been shot up and left. Gilbert thought that I was the police coming in. He wasn't going to jail, he told me. To which I thought was a wonderful idea. So he fired right into her head. Once I got her wrapped up and put into the bedroom with her sister who was still alive as well, I took care of him." Edmond asked her if she thought he should know how she'd done that. "No. Let's just say what they saw in there is nothing at all as to what the living room looked like when she was finished with him."

"And the girls?" She told him that Selma had been lying in her doorway with a bullet to her head, and she'd been able to heal her quickly. But it had taken her a bit longer, and that was why Harley had been hurt, too. "Do you think that there will be any kind of payback? For keeping the girls alive? I mean, they, whoever it was that gave us this, they're not going to make us choose someone else to die because of what we'd done here today?"

"No. I believe, and it is really hard to believe, that you and I were chosen to do this deed for the families of those saved. At some point? I don't know. Maybe we'll be around long enough to see what purpose they were to serve because we saved them both.

Chapter 1

Summer didn't know a thing about looking into purchasing a house. How to make an offer on one, or even to know what questions to ask when it was time to put in one. As it was right now, all she knew about any house was that it was necessary and that it needed bathrooms. The house that she and her daughters had lived in was given to them by the government, and there had been no picking out carpet or bedroom furniture, nor did she get to decide what size refrigerator they needed. It was there to use, and that was what she'd used.

"There are five bedrooms on the second floor, including the master bedroom." The woman with her, Shelly something, had been with her throughout the entire house-hunting experience. When she saw Ayden coming through the front door, she turned to go to him to figure out what the hell he'd been thinking in asking her to look at the house.

"I don't know anything about this place." He took a step back, and she thought about how she must have looked running up to him the way that she had. "The girls love this one because of the pool and the fenced-in back yard. I might have told them that we'd get a dog one of these days if we had a house and a yard."

"A dog would be good for the two of them as it would know to keep them safe. As for buying a house? I know less than you do. At least you know what should be in one that doesn't have a half dozen men living in it and messing things up." She'd forgotten that he'd lived with his brothers his entire life. "What do you think about this house? Anywhere you want, you can have a pool and fenced-in back yard. Also, there are things that can be fixed. I only know that because of my brother's home. Things that are outdated can be taken care of as well."

"I told the girls that. They don't want to give me any chance to change my mind about the place." He asked her if she'd done that before. " Change my mind? Sure, what parent hasn't? But I think they were thinking that if the pool is here now, I can't tell them that we can't afford it when summer rolls around. Same with the dog. I want to get them one...what does that have to do with your brother and him being the alpha? A great deal, I'm betting."

"Yes, they're all loyal to him. Not as much to us, but they'll die to protect anyone that he tells them to. As for the pool? I guess I can see that." She knew that she was his mate. What did that entail? She didn't know. There had been enough information about mates around that she had an idea that they were supposed to be together forever. However, she'd been with a man before and didn't much trust the forever bullshit. "I'm sorry I'm late, but there was trouble at the house we're using to store things for people in need."

Last night, Ayden told her that he couldn't work around meat, eat it, or do anything else that had to do with beef or the like. Mostly, it was red meat, and he told her why. It sort of made her ill to think about it as well, and she'd not even been around when it had happened.

Ayden had been helping out Brandy by trying to see why the restaurant that she was supposed to invest in was losing money. He'd been an undercover dishwasher for a week when he found out that they were serving him dead body meat rather than the meat that had come from the slaughterhouse like his brother had been working on. He'd been sick since. Every time he thought of having a nice steak, even his wolf would have a belly ache and then nightmares on top of that.

It made her sick to think how people treated other people who would just kill them and serve them up on the menu like they were nothing. She'd yet to tell her daughters, but then she didn't know that she would either. It was just too much to put on a couple of eight year old kids.

"What do you think of this place?" Ayden told her that he liked the yard and the fenced-in part of it. But he didn't know anything about the kitchen. He could cook, he told her, but he'd never had his own place where he might want to cook for several people. "I guess I can see that too. My daughters aren't all that picky, but they do have choices in mind when it comes to feeding them."

"I've never fed a little girl, so you're up on that for me, too." She nodded, and they headed to the kitchen. There was something about the big room that she did not care for. It wasn't until Ayden joined her in the room that it occurred to her. "What do you mean? It's not very large. It seems large enough to me."

"Think of this room with the four of us in it trying to get ready for school. I'm assuming since your brother has staff, we might have a cook, too. I'm not saying that I'm there with you yet, I don't even know if I like you all that much, but it would be hard to get around with food and getting them out the door while in here in time for school or whatever else they might have going on. No, I don't care for the kitchen. And that reminds me, your brother told me that he filed it with the city that the two of us are married and that you adopted the girls. I've not told them yet, but he said you'd understand. I don't know that I like that anymore than I do this kitchen."

"He did that because of your in-laws. Did you know that the Fortrights want to take the girls from you?" It was the first that she'd heard about it. "Brandy found the couple, and the police let them know that their son was dead. And in that, they told her about the girls. I don't know if it was supposed to be a secret or not, but they know now and think that it's all your fault that Gilbert is dead."

"Are you going to be like this forever? Just saying what you want without any lead-up?" He looked at her, confused. "You might well have worked your way up to that. I don't know, maybe they said that they wanted to meet their granddaughters and then come up with…you know what? I don't want that either. You leading up to things. I'd rather you just tell me what's going on so that I'm not blindsided. I'm sorry. Yes, I want to have it out in the open when you tell me something. And no, I didn't know that they wanted the girls." She thought of her in-laws. "They never seemed to want to have anything to do with them before. I wonder why they do now."

"I have no idea, as I've never met any of them. But as for telling you straight up, I can do that for you. And just so you know, I'd like to have my information that way as well. I don't like beating around the bush for things." He helped get the girls out of the back yard and into the car.

The girls seemed to like Ayden more than they did her most of the time, anyway. After getting them loaded into the car and on the road, she was set to go to another house on the list of houses she was to look at.

She'd been living in federally subsidized homes before her ex-husband Gilbert had been killed last week. She found out that when he'd been watching his own kids—thinking that he needed to be paid to do so, he'd been dealing drugs from her place while having her children locked in their rooms or bathroom. One of her daughters, Selma, had been shot while the deal was going down, and without the help of Mac, one of Ayden's sisters-in-law, and her magic, she might well have lost her.

Sometimes, it was too much to think about, others she just couldn't believe how lucky she was that she'd found her mate in Ayden, who had come with a very caring and loving bunch of men. Their size only made her nervous, but she was never afraid of them, however.

Summer owed so much to this family that she wasn't sure that she was ever going to pay them back. As it was now, all she wanted to do was find herself a nice dark corner and cry herself into a stupor. Now, because of Gilbert, she could no longer stay at the house that had made it so that they had a roof over her head. Summer needed to find herself someplace to stay with them, or they were going to be homeless. However that worked with having a new husband that she didn't know all that well and two little girls that meant the world to her. Life was too complicated right now.

"I don't like this house." She looked up at the house and decided that she didn't care for it either, the same as Harley said. Someone had painted it black, and it had black shutters, too. Even the windows looked like they were too dark, and she didn't want to get out to look at it. "It looks like a monster house that Gilbert used to tell us about that he was going to sell us to."

That was another thing. They didn't call their dad 'dad' anymore. She was positive that they'd not been calling him that for a while, but she couldn't put her finger on when it had started. Not that it mattered to her. She never liked the bastard anyway.

Ayden didn't even try to talk them into seeing the house but told them to re-buckle, and they started toward the last house on the list they'd been given. She didn't like house hunting, she thought, any more than she did job hunting. It was just too much work.

The last house on their list didn't look any better than the one they'd just left. She wanted it finished with. A place where they didn't have to pick up their sleeping bags nightly and then move them all around the next evening when they went to bed again. Living in a hotel like they were right now had its advantages, but they were few and far in between. She wanted, like a lot of things of late, finished so that she could move on with the rest of her life. One where she had a job, money in the bank, and her little girls were safe and sound. Summer wondered if that was going to happen.

"Here's one." She was brought out of her musing when Ayden spoke. "It's for sale by owner. While I know what the words mean, I have no idea why that's different from having a realtor try to sell you one. But we can have a look at it if you're willing." She nodded, just wanting to get off her feet when they pulled into the big circular driveway. "It looks big enough for you guys, don't you think?"

"There's a pool too. See it?" Getting out of the car, she looked at the big place. It more than likely had too many bedrooms, and she wasn't going to be able to do anything but clean house all day. The girls could have their own bedrooms, but it would be a lot of work to keep them up. Even if it had a pool, someone had to take care of that as well. "Mommy, look, there's a big barn out back too. We can have a tractor."

Summer didn't know what the attraction was about a tractor, but the girls had been talking about it all morning. She did wonder if Ayden had said something about mowing the lawn, and that was where it had come from, but she just didn't care. The sooner they could get back to the hotel, and she could put her feet up, the better. She was beginning to hate herself with all her whining, she realized. Putting a smile on her face, even if she didn't mean it, made her feel just a little better.

She wasn't even sure why she was so exhausted today. It had been wonderful sleeping on a good mattress, one that didn't have lumps in it that were older than her. The girls were perfectly fine with sleeping on the floor, the room only had one bed in it, and for now, that was all they had. She'd had a long hot shower and a good breakfast, but she was so exhausted that she was sure that she could fall asleep at any second. Getting out of the car with the others, she leaned against it to have a look around.

It *would* require a tractor to mow the lawn.

But she could almost see herself doing it. She'd never once mowed anything and didn't know why the thought of it appealed to her, but it was suddenly all she could think about. Mowing and caring for the lawn. She could almost see a tree for Christmas in the front window with those blow-up things all around the yard. Shaking her head, she went to meet the people who seemed to be in charge of showing the house.

Not only did the house have a nice sized pool, but there was a pool house as well. In addition to that, there was the barn that held not just a tractor but snowmobiles as well. She'd not even seen the inside of the house, the kitchen mostly, and she had herself living here and getting old with Ayden. Her mind was mush right now, and she didn't know where any of these weird thoughts were coming from.

The living room was large. Larger than her old place by half, she'd bet. The fireplace had been running when they went into the house, but instead of it having to have logs to keep it going, there was gas coming into the house that would keep the room toasty all winter long. Summer hated that she was going to have to be going into the kitchen now. She just knew that it was going to be the worst kitchen that she'd ever seen. But that didn't happen as it turned out. As soon as she walked in, Summer wanted to tell the people who lived in the house to go away. She'd found her dream home.

The Bradshaws, the owners of the house, were very nice people. Allowing the girls to wander around in the back yard that was indeed fenced in. But they also made them some hot cocoa and cookies so that they could sit in the living room with them while they talked about the house. She had to admit, she was impressed with the questions that her girls had asked, thinking that knowing what sort of heat the house had— gas, was a good one. Also, how new the roof was from Ayden. Apparently, they'd been watching renovation shows on television and knew the kind of questions that had been taken care of on the shows.

Before she knew it, they were headed out the door with an offer in on the house and headed to the bank to see if they could get a loan. It was done and finished, a saying her grannie used to say before the ink was dried on the paperwork.

She had a house to move into now.

"How about some dinner before I drop you off at the hotel?" Ayden had been coming by to see them at least twice a day since they moved into the hotel. The government was picking up the tab, he'd told her for their help in getting a man like Gilbert and his cohorts off the streets. There was going to be a bonus of sorts, too, that she'd get for helping get the criminals caught who had been selling drugs to the high school for some time now. "We can do pizza, or we can celebrate that you have a house now and are having something fun, too."

"Fun." Of course, the girls wanted fun. She honestly didn't care so long as she didn't have to cook or clean up. Something was the matter with her, and she was going to have to see someone about it soon. This was just crazy that she wanted to do nothing but sleep.

"I've spoken to my brothers about why you're feeling off the way that you are." She asked him why he'd do that. "You asked me why you were so exhausted, and I went to them. They're the only people I know who might have an answer. But it was Mac that I think figured it out. She said that you were now in a place where you feel safe and sound, and the girls aren't going to be hurt, and your body is just wanting to take advantage of the help. I don't know if it's true or not, but it sounds like something that seems right. What do you think?"

"I don't know." But she did think about it. "You know, you could be right. I have been sleeping better, but I'm still tired. I bet you're right."

The four of them ended up eating at a restaurant that did have a kids' menu, too. It was a burger place, of course, but it had pizzas and subs that the other joint didn't. She just wanted a nice big salad and was pleasantly surprised that they had taco salad, something that she'd not had in ages. Her daughters both had subs, too, but each of them was different. While they loved to have hot subs, they didn't care for spicy. Ayden had a taco salad with her but without meat. She almost felt sorry for him in his aversions.

He spoke to his brother Lica more than anyone, but when they were just getting their food, he and his wife showed up. She didn't know the other woman all that well and was slightly intimidated by her. While she knew that she was something higher on the food chain about being an alpha bitch, that was the extent of her knowledge about what the couple did.

"The house is going to need a bit of work, as you were told." The girls decided that they wanted to know all the details, and she didn't turn them down when they asked when they could move in. "It'll be after Thanksgiving, that's for sure, but they think they can be out by Christmas. Since you don't have much in the way of furniture, I'm thinking that you guys can be in there with a tree up in time for Santa Claus."

The furnace had to be replaced and was going to be started on in the morning. Also, the air conditioning on the second floor needed to be updated. She was fine with that, and so were the girls. What she didn't know was what they were going to do for the next month while they waited for the house to be ready.

"I have a couple of rentals that you can stay in. They're sort of furnished but not with much. If you fall in love with the things there, you're more than welcome to them. Also, I know that there are several houses that I own that you can pick and choose from them as well in the way of things you might need."

"Bedroom sets for the girls most of all. Other than that, I can't think of much else. I just want them to be able to sleep well." Brandy said that she could handle that for them as she wanted to give them a welcome gift from the family. "You don't have to do that. I'm sure they can use the sleeping bags until they're ready."

"Nonsense. They're welcome here, and we're happy to have them as part of the family. I believe that Ayden's grandmother is going to get them computers so that they can keep up with their homework, too." It was all too much, and she said as much to her. "We have money, which means that you have it as well. I won't spoil them, for as much as I'd like to but there are things that we can do for them in light of how they have been treated. Besides, they're my first nieces, and I want to have a bit of fun with them."

"I don't want them to be able to come to you when they want something, and I've told them no." Brandy told her that she'd never do that. Not ever. That her word was what they would always go by. "Thank you for that."

~*~

Ayden hadn't ever wanted a woman like he did Summer. It was as if she was the only woman in the world for him, and he didn't know how to react. As soon as they were settled at the hotel, he found himself a room to stay in, too, and was just settling down when Harley called him on the cell phone he'd gotten for them both. He never wanted them to feel unsafe or that they couldn't get in touch with him. He also wanted them to be able to talk to him anytime they had questions about being in a family of wolves.

"Mr. Ayden, I have a question for you. Well, Selma and I have a question for you. What is it we're supposed to call you? I know we've been calling you Mr. Ayden, but that's not very much fun. Can we call you Ayden?" He told her that it was all right with him, but she had to ask her mom. "She said that we had to ask you. We already call your brothers uncle and their wives aunt so it's good that we call you by your first name. We've not called our dad, Gilbert, Dad in a very long time. He never liked us all that much anyway."

"I already love you." She said that they loved him too but were waiting on their mom. "Yes, I can understand that. Waiting on your mom is a good thing since she seems to be so stressed out."

"I don't think she's stressed so much as she's wigged out." Ayden laughed and then asked her what that meant. "She told us that she's waiting for the other shoe to drop. I kinda know what that means, but I think with the grandparents wanting us, she's freaking out a little bit on that too."

"If they try anything, I want you to know that my family and I will protect you with our lives. They'll never harm you so long as I have blood in my body." She told him that was sweet, but nobody ever meant that. "I do. With all my heart. I will not allow them to touch you, and if they do, then I'm going to make them regret ever being born."

She didn't say anything for several minutes, and he let her think about it. They'd never had much of a father figure, and their mother had been working all the time to keep them in food and clothing. He was going to make sure that they had everything they needed for as long as he lived. When she finally spoke again, he smiled.

"Can we see your wolf?" He said that it would be his pleasure to show her and, in fact, thought that they should get to know all the wolves in his family. "That would be good. I know that you're bigger than a regular wolf, but since neither of us has seen one, then we have nothing to compare it to."

He laughed. He didn't know why he thought that was so funny, but it felt good to be able to laugh. Selma said she thought he was goofy. Ayden told her that he could be when it suited him, but it had been a long time since he'd laughed like that.

"I'm sorry that you don't get to laugh all that much." She then asked about his family. "You don't have parents around, do you? Uncle Lica said that they were terrible people and that we were lucky that we didn't get to see them. Is that true?"

"Yes, my mom is in prison for killing my dad. They had a plan to make it so that we all died, and they could be without us. They beat the six of us and blamed us for everything that went wrong in their lives. I hate them both. The two of them would beat us daily, nearly killing us simply because they could. And they never liked your uncle Lica for some reason." Both girls told him that they were sorry. "I am as well. That's why I'm not terribly good at being around other people. I don't know what they want from me. I don't trust all that much like your mother doesn't. I'm hoping that I can get over that soon. But for some reason, not only do I trust the two of you, but I trust your mother as well. With all my being."

"We'll never make you not trust us, Ayden, I promise you." He had to fight the tears that started to fall down his cheeks. "Good night, Ayden. Thank you for being there for us. I don't know what we would have done had your family not helped us when we needed it most. See you in the morning."

The sun was just coming up in the sky when he got out of his bed. It was nice having a room so close to his new family, and he wanted to wake up daily and have a meal with the three of them. It was something new for him to have a family of his own, and he was going to make sure that he treated them right every moment of every day.

By the end of the day, he was exhausted again. Spending time with the girls as their mother had found herself a job and was glad to be working, he took them to the mall, as pitiful as it was to find them some clothing. They still couldn't get into the house they'd been renting as it was still a crime scene, but that didn't mean that they didn't need things from the place. After shopping all day, glad for his grannie's help, he was ready to take a long nap and not wake up until morning again.

"You'll have to have things that most people don't think about when buying their first home with children—especially girls in the house." She told him that he'd need things like dressers and furniture for the little girls but also things like hangers to hang their things up with. "Towels for them as well as little girl things that they'll need to have a bath with, too. I never thought of that until I had a look around in their hotel. My goodness, they're very neat little girls, aren't they?"

"I don't know." He didn't know anything much about them. Honest with his grannie, she told him that he needed to get with the other women in the household and have them take Summer shopping for them all. "Like, what kind of things are you talking about? Soap and shampoo I get, but what little girl things will they need?" It hit him like a brick when he got it. "Oh. Oh."

"Yes, I'm sure you're getting it now. With a houseful of women, you're going to have to be less embarrassed about things than you are right now. If you think of it as embarrassing, they're not going to be able to go to you because they won't want you to dislike them." He said that he'd get some books on things for teenage little girls. "You do that, but I'd ask their mother too. You don't have to run right out now and figure it out, but you will need to be prepared if they need you."

Ayden didn't know what to think when he went to the library to check out some books on raising little girls. He felt like a pervert when he opened the first book and had to slam it shut when he saw what it was talking about. Women were a mystery to him, and he was hoping that someday, he'd be able to give his brothers advice on how to get through this part of their lives. Periods and development were things that he'd never thought about in all his life, having to talk to someone, his own daughters, about with their mother. Thank goodness for her in their lives, he thought.

They were still living out of bags from the store when they found a rental that they could live in for a while. It was only a month, but it seemed like forever to them all. After talking with Summer and her telling him that she'd had the sex talk with the girls, he could have laid down at her feet and begged for the same information. Ayden was going to be a good dad to the two girls even if he had to read every book there was on adolescents. He only hoped that someday they'd be able to talk to him like their mother did to him. Christ, he wasn't going to survive this if he kept feeling his face heat up whenever he was around them.

Moving them into the house they were going to rent was an eye-opener too. While Harley was tomboyish, Selma was all girl. The house that they were renting had two little girl beds, but one was a canopy bed, which Selma wanted, and Harley took the one done up in horses and farm animals. He was excited to watch them grow up into personalities.

Chapter 2

Clive set the phone in the receiver and looked around the room. Rose asked him what he'd been able to find out, and all he did was stare at her. She had to know better than to ask him questions when he was in charge of things today.

"You bring that attitude to me, mister, and I'll slap you fucking sideways." He'd forgotten just for a second who he was dealing with and the day of the week. He told her what he knew. "What do you mean you can't find them? What's the point of having money if you can't use it to find people. Did you tell that man what we want?"

"I did. He seems to think that they've left the little town they were in. Since Gilbert and that Summer person were together, we've known where that person is. You'd think with two kids hanging at her tit that we'd be able to locate them after she killed our son." It wasn't as if they liked Gilbert, but that wasn't the point. The point was they were without any living relatives but the brats, and they were going to get them. At least one of them. "Once the body was removed from that house, they seemed to have vanished like the prom queen's virginity on homecoming night."

That sounded better in his head, but he didn't correct himself. Rose would go on about how he didn't need to say a word without her permission. Today was her day to be in charge, and he hated that almost as much as he hated his wife. But they had things going the way that they wanted now, and there was no point in messing up a good thing.

The two of them had been married for nearly forty years. Neither of them had wanted to get married, but it was that, or they'd lose all their fortune — though they had lost it anyway. His parents had arranged the marriage, and he was to do it, or there would be no money. Also, they were to have a child as part of the deal. Clive looked at his wife and mentally shook his head. They'd worked out well, the two of them, so long as they followed their own set of rules.

On Monday, Wednesday, and Friday, he was the one that made decisions. On Tuesday,

Thursday and Saturday, Rose would make them. Sunday they neither one made any kind of decisions, and that had suited them just fine all their married life. There were rules too to those decisions. There was no overruling the decision from the day before; you couldn't just keep going back over the same decisions daily because once they were made, they stuck.

The decision-making rules applied to everything. Money, household things, and even what they watched on television that night. Right now, they were watching a game show, and he was fine with that. But he never let on that he enjoyed her decisions either. Clive was sure that she did the same to him. They coexisted, and that was all they'd ever wanted out of their deal of being husband and wife.

"Did you find out where they're staying or just that they're not in the house anymore? I don't like that the government is so willy-nilly about things. They should be able to tell us whatever we want to know as we pay our taxes, too. That bitch had better play ball with us, or so help me, Clive, I'm going to make her regret ever being around our son." He was reasonably sure that she did that anyway but kept that to himself. Gilbert had been a handful before they'd sent him away to military school.

Not that it helped. He'd become more violent as the years went by, and when he'd knocked that Summer person around and she'd allowed herself to get knocked up, he didn't seem to worry about how that was going to make them look either. They had a reputation to uphold, and he made them look bad. That was why having the brats was so important. They needed, now more than ever, someone to take over the family business when it was time. They had that all worked out as well. As soon as they were to get the girls or just one, he didn't care. They were going to make sure that she was healthy, then send her off to boarding school where they'd not have to deal with her. He wanted nothing to do with raising a child, not even his own child, when it came to it.

"Did you hear me?" He looked at Rose when she snapped her fingers in front of his face. "I asked you if you have any information on who was the one that pulled the trigger on Gilbert?"

"The police. That's all I was told that the police had had to take him down because he was holding a gun to one of the girls' heads. I don't understand why they didn't just let him kill one of the girls. It certainly would have made our lives better, but there you have it. No one knows who pulled the killing trigger." She asked him where the body was. "We can't get it until we claim it. Silly thing if you ask me. It's not like anyone is going to claim his body anyway. Just let us have it so that we can find out who the killer was and take care of them for killing our son. Do you suppose that there is more than one bullet in his body, and that's what they're holding onto it?"

"I never thought of that. Yes, that could be it. If so, then we'll have the entire force put out of business by suing them. Is it too much to ask that someone pay for his death? Even if it's the police? I tell you, Clive, people get stupider every day if you ask me. The rich are the only ones that have any sense." Not that they were rich. Daily, they were borrowing from Paul to pay Peter. As it was right now, they barely had enough money to go to the end of the year. They'd never been any good at saving money, and it was beginning to show nowadays. "What do you know of that insurance policy that we had on Gilbert? Can it be cashed in yet?"

"I told you yesterday that without us making the payments, then it's not any good. They told me that when it was my turn." She told him that she'd forgotten. "I don't understand that either. As far as I know, my parents never paid on their insurance, yet we were able to collect on it when they were dead. Why do you have to pay on a policy only to have to cash it in when they're dead? Makes no sense at all."

"Something about paying into it so that we can get a return. Stupid people. If I had the money to pay for it, why on earth would I need to cash in the policy in the first place? If I were in charge, that's the way that I'd make it. You just had insurance on everybody."

He didn't know how that would work either but kept his mouth shut. Besides, it gave him a headache trying to figure out how businesses worked. That was another reason they were so broke all the time. They didn't understand people and the workings of their businesses.

Neither of them owned a cell phone, and there wasn't a computer in the house that they used. The two of them, when necessary, would use the old landline in their home rather than try and figure out how the other things worked. The staff — what little there was left, he knew, had phones on them all the time. He'd hear them twitter once in a while and they'd wander off. He liked the olden days, where men were men and women knew how to keep their mouths shut. That was another thing that he'd not mention to his wife. She'd knock him three ways from Sunday, as his daddy used to say.

"The phone is ringing." Picking it up as there wasn't enough money to have a butler anymore, he answered it with a bark of his name. "Clive, don't tell them who they got. Darn it, man, don't you get anything right?"

"Mr. Clive Forthright, my name is Ayden Frazier. I wanted to ask you some questions." He told him that he wasn't buying anything. "Not that you could afford it, but that's not what I wanted. I'm calling about my wife and our family."

"I don't know you from crap. Stop calling here." The man said something, and he had to have him repeat it. "What do you mean, you've adopted my granddaughters. No, that's not right. That Summer person has them, and we're going to have to get one of them from her since she killed off our son."

"Your son was killed by the police department and the feds. It's against the law to sell drugs on high school property and also to have drugs and prostitution run from a government housing." He told the man that he didn't know what he was talking about. "Oh, but I do know. And I wanted to give you a heads-up that you're not going to take my daughters away from me. If I find you within fifty feet of them, I'm going to rip your throat out. I've been doing some digging on your family, and it seems like you knew what Gilbert was up to. Even going so far as to profit from his dealings."

"We needed the money. A son should take care of his parents. That's what we had to do when my parents decided to retire." He wished he'd not said that, but the man was talking in riddles. "Why do I give a good fig about your daughters. I'm going to talk to that Summer person about her giving one of them to us so that our family name has a good standing."

"That Summer person, as you call her, is my wife, and her daughters are now mine." He told the man that was impossible. He'd never given permission for her to get married. "She's a grown woman and doesn't need your permission to do anything. As for the girls, you're not going to touch one of them either. They're mine now."

Not knowing how to deal with the man, he handed the phone to Rose. Before she could get more than just saying her name, she was listening to his bull crap too. What did he mean by saying that he was going to adopt them? Or did he say that he had adopted them? The man was making no sense at all, and he didn't want to deal with him right now. Then he listened to his wife.

"You've no right to do that. I didn't give you permission to marry her, and that's my final word on the situation. Now. Here is what you're going to do, young man. You're going to—" She must have been cut off because the next thing he knew, Rose was sputtering about while the man was shouting. He could hear him from across the room. "Now you see here. I'm not going to allow you to—" She'd been cut off again. The man had no manners, was all he could think about. And he was messing with the wrong person if he cut his wife off one more time.

When the phone was put back in the cradle,

the two of them stared at one another. They'd never been so disrespected in their life and in their own home, too. Getting up, he bellowed toward the kitchen that he needed some tea right now. Hearing the glass break gave him a good start, but he laughed too. Sitting back in his chair, he finally asked Rose what had happened.

"He told me that he's not going to give up one of the children. How does he get off telling me what he's going to be doing? Not to mention telling me that I'm going to be going to jail, too. Did you know that it was against the law for us to be profiting off of what Gilbert was doing? I think you might well have told me, but I don't—he cut me off, the little pisser. Cut me off like I wasn't talking to him." He told her that he'd done the same to him. "Well, I'm not going to put up with it. Do you still have people at the station house? You get on them right now to go and arrest that man for being rude to me."

"I don't know that that is going to work." He explained to her how the man was right about what he was saying. "What do you mean he's right that we can't profit off of our own son. Darn it, Clive, I don't like this, not one bit. It's my turn, and it should be the way that I want it to be."

"I know, and I don't either. Here we were having a nice evening, and he calls here, making threats. It didn't even matter to him that he was talking to the one in charge of today, Rose. That's no way to treat us." She patted him on the head, and then they both shut up when the maid brought them their tea. Rose grabbed her arm before she could leave. "See that you write down what you broke too, or I'm going to know what for."

By the time his tea was cooled off enough for him to drink, he was upset again. The man had done this to them, and he was going to have to take a stand or do something against him. Picking up the phone when Rose told him to call the station house, he was just about ready to scream when the man put him on hold to go to his office.

"You answer the phone so we can talk when I call there. I don't like being put on hold." The man told him that he didn't know he'd been going to call. "That's not my problem. You shouldn't be out fraternizing with your employees anyway. My taxes paid up means you work for me."

"Mr. Forthright, I don't know if you're aware of this or not, but everyone pays their taxes and expects me to do what they want. You're not any different than Ms. Shawl, who lives in the housing place along Meadow Drive." He felt his anger surge up. Imagine comparing him to those people on Meadow Drive. "Now, you don't want to be messing with the Frazier boys. They got themselves some money now, and I don't think there is a person in his town who doesn't owe them boys something for helping them out. You and your missus, you just leave that Ayden alone with his family, and we'll get along just fine."

"He isn't going to turn over one of his daughters." The officer told him that was a good thing as they weren't to be separated. "That Summer person has had them all their lives, and now it's time she gave up one of them. The better one of them, too. I won't be taking the stupid one just because she has two to choose from. I got myself no use for girls, but that's all she had, so that's going to have to do for us."

"Mr. Forthright, if you try and take one of those pretty little girls, there is going to be hell to pay. Not just from the police, but those Fraziers take care of what's theirs, and they'll kill you if you try anything stupid." He said that it was only fair. "Fair or not, you touch one of them girls, and I'm going to turn my back on them so that they can deal with parents' justice."

"You see here now. I want you to go out to that shanty that they live in and take one of them right now. It's only fair since you killed off my son. He wasn't much anyway, but he was a Forthright, and I want justice for him." He told him that he wasn't going to do that. "Then why am I even talking to you."

After hanging up, he picked up the receiver and redialed the number. He thought maybe he'd get a different person, one that would work with him, but it was the same voice. He did that sort of thing when he had to call things like the cable company. If you didn't like what they were telling you, simply hang up only to call back, and you'd get another person. Not that he believed any of them were in the area. They were all calling from some third-world country, and he was upset about it.

His tea was now cold, and he didn't have anything to eat either. The television had long since gone to something else, and he and Rose were talking about how ridiculous everyone was being about that Summer person. What right did she have to do any of the things that she'd been doing? None, that was it.

His head was pounding so hard he knew that if he didn't get to lie down soon, he was going to be sick. There was nothing worse than being sick, he thought. Getting up, he was headed to bed when his front doorbell rang. Going to see who it was, he was surprised to find someone in a suit standing there. He asked him what he wanted.

"My name is Federal Marshall James Calhoun, and I'm here to question you about the involvement you have had with your son in his endeavors to sell drugs to minors around town." He told him what he had told the other man. They needed the money. "So you're telling me that you knew what he was doing and have profited off of his illegal activities."

"Don't be stupid. Of course, we did. How else were we to make any money with our taxes being paid and the house in good repair. If you need to be bribed, you go and talk to that man at the head of my son's operation. His name was…let me see." He turned to Rose and asked her as she was headed up the stairs, too. "Peter Conklin. He's the one in charge of the dope going around here. And he was nice enough to bring us the money too when there was enough profit. Now, it's nearly nine o'clock, and we're headed to bed. If you want any more answers—now see here. What do you think you're doing?"

He was put in cuffs along with his wife. As they were being led out to a cruiser, he yelled at his neighbors to mind their own business. They were forever standing out on the street, watching whatever was going on. He remembered once when they threw a party for the street when his son was put in jail. Ingrates. All of them were ingrates. Who did that sort of thing?

~*~

While he knew what was going on with the Fortrights, he didn't have a great many details. They'd been arrested last night in full view of their neighbors. Ayden even got to see some of the video when they'd been trying to get away from the men that had come to arrest them. Laughing, he looked over at his daughter—how he loved to say that—and sobered up when she glared at him.

"It's rude to have fun at someone else's expense, Ayden." He told her what he knew and didn't hold back when he told her about how they'd been going to take one of them. "Take us where? Mom would have had a fit if they'd tried that."

"They wouldn't have gotten in the front door, I promise you. But they also admitted to knowing that your biological father was selling drugs to teenagers on the high school grounds." She said that they used to come by the house when he was there, and he'd sell them to them, too. "He was a terrible man, and I'm happy to have them out of your lives. Both of them are now saying that it's your mom's fault that Gilbert is dead and that they expect for her to turn one of you, the better of the two of you, over to them so that their good names are still intact."

"I'm not going anywhere with them, and neither is Harley." He told Selma that he knew that, too. "I wonder what they would have done had they gotten one of us? They wouldn't have had an easy time of it is what Brandy said. Did we tell you that she's having us go to self-defense classes? I think we need that more than ever."

"They're in jail now, honey, and it doesn't look as if they're going to be getting out anytime too soon." She asked if, because they were old, people would feel sorry for them and let them go. "I don't think so. I believe most of their neighbors are happy that they're gone, too. Something happened there, and I've not been made aware of it yet, but they're going to be gone a long time."

"I hope so." Harley joined them in the kitchen, the house was starting to look like a used box outlet. They'd been finding things all over the place in town at auctions and garage sales. There weren't too many of those this time of year, however. "Thanksgiving is next Thursday. What did you want to do about taking a covered dish?"

"I don't think that we're supposed to do that now. Aunt Brandy said she was going to have it catered so that no one has to clean up. Did you know that a turkey takes forever to cook? I guess on account of it having big boobs."

"Turkeys do have big boobs." He thought about the conversations he'd been having since he'd found out he was a father. It never ceased to amaze him what sort of things they could ask questions about, either. And nothing was off limits. When they'd spent the day at the slaughterhouse with Lica, they had more questions than he thought a book might. And they read everything they could get their hands on, too. Christ, he was having so much fun.

Ayden helped the girls make placards for the table. It had cost him the world to get enough glitter and glue so that they would have enough to go around. Even as they were drying, all he could think about was how much glitter was going to be in the rental until the end of time. He was glad it was here and not his own home that they were being crafty with.

"Ayden, what do you know about sex?" He nearly swallowed his tongue when Selma asked him that question. "I don't want you to explain it to me. Mom already did, but you do know that's how babies come, right?"

"I do know that, yes I do." He eyed her hard. "Did one of my brothers ask you to talk to me about sex with you? I'm going to murder them, just so you know."

"No, they didn't say anything. But Aunt Brandy is getting big, and we were wondering if you and Mom were going to have any children. Besides us? I want a little brother." He wasn't sure what to tell her about that. "You and Mom sleep in different houses. I hope you know that won't get us a brother or a sister if you keep doing that. I think you like each other, but we're wondering if we're going to be only children." He wasn't even going to question her about being an only child when she had a twin sister.

"Yes, I'm aware of that. But your mom is still trying to figure things out." She told him that she thought Mom knew about sex, too. He felt his face heat up hotter. "I'm sure she does. But you see, she has had a lot done to her in the last month or so, and I'm waiting on her to make the decision where I'm going to be sleeping."

It wasn't nice of him at all to put the blame on Summer, but he didn't want to have this conversation with one of her daughters. It wasn't as bad as how come bulls had balls and cows didn't, but it was right up there. He decided right then and there that he was going to not say a word to his brothers on about raising little girls. He was going to let them figure it out all on their own, and he was going to sit back and laugh at them. At the very least, he was going to be laughing at his own home so they'd not hurt him. Ayden thought that he'd write down some of the questions that the girls had so that he could tell them to ask their parents. Yes, he was enjoying it to a point about having the oldest children, but also not. Christ, he was terrified of what sort of questions a son would ask when and if they ever had one.

When Summer came home, he could tell that something had happened. Getting her to tell him took a while, but he found out that she didn't want to work anymore. He was all for that, he told her. He missed her when she was away.

"What will we do for money then?" He told her that he had a job that paid well. "What is it you do anyway? I don't think that I've ever found out."

"I go to businesses that need a boost up and see what I can see about helping them. It might be that they have the wrong sort of boxes to send things out. They might have too many employees or not enough. I study the place for a while, and then when I get it figured out, I tell Brandy about it. She decides then if she thinks that the place can benefit from having more money or just close up." Summer asked him if it paid well. "It really does. I get paid very well, and I've only been banking it so that we can have a nest egg for ourselves. The house is paid off; it was a deal that Brandy made with all of us, and we were to get a house from her. I did let you know that Brandy is wealthy, didn't I?"

"Yes, you did." Summer made them all quick sandwiches before she sat down herself. "I don't want to work. At least not as hard as I have been. I miss you and the kids."

"We miss you as well." After handing out juice bottles and napkins, he sat down with them all as well. "Brandy had found us a cook. She said that she hired us one because she didn't want to see you in the kitchen all the time when you could be out with her. I think that she needs friends like you to keep her out of trouble. Though, now that I think about it, you're trouble too."

He kissed her on her nose and got up to get himself a fork. There was potato salad in one of the containers, and he loved that more than he did any other salad that was with the stuff they were eating.

After lunch, he went back to his office. He had to fill out the forms that Brandy had set up for him so that she could check the boxes of the places he worked. There were a lot of questions that he had to ask and fill out, but he enjoyed the job now that he knew he wasn't going to be going undercover for her. That had gotten both him and his wolf really sick recently.

He'd been working for a restaurant over the summer, and they'd served him human remains for his dinner. He'd been eating there nightly, and it never occurred to him what he might be eating. Their plan had been to make him a part of the deal they had going, selling off the real meat and then serving the customers human remains to boost the profits they were making off the sale of the other meats. Ayden had been sick since and had not been able to eat any red meat, nor had his wolf. He hoped that he'd be able to get over it soon, but he just didn't know. It was a great deal to process.

"Ayden." He looked at Selma when she said his name and smiled at her. She was by and far the most girly girl he knew, and he loved her for it. Harley was the exact opposite in that she was the most tomboyish little girl he'd ever met. Yet the two of them seemed to get along. "Ayden, what if I told you that I could see the dead. What would you do?"

Chapter 3

Selma knew that she was being strange, but she didn't know what else to do. Brandy had taken her aside last week and told her that she'd saved her life by giving her a bit of magic. Not asking her if that meant that she could see the ghosts around, she nodded and told her that she'd try things out to see what it gave her. So far, it had only been the ability to change her clothing and to see the ghosts, of course. She'd rather have to change her own clothing than to see the others that seemed to be around everywhere.

"What do you mean when you say you can see ghosts?" She glared at Ayden, wondering how else there was to see ghosts everywhere she went. "I'm sorry. I don't know...tell me what you mean, and I'll try to help you. I guess the next question would be...I'm sorry. I'm not sure what I can do to help you out with this."

"Do normal people see ghosts? Don't

answer that." She looked out the window that was in his office and asked him what he saw when he looked at her. "I mean, do you see this freak or something?"

"Okay, you're not a freak. If you can see ghosts, it's something that we deal with. No name calling even if it's you that is doing that." She nodded and looked at him, her eyes filling with tears. "If you cry right now, I'm going to be a mess. I want to help you with—did you tell your mom? Or anyone else?"

"Harley knows. Nobody else. I wanted to tell Brandy. She said that when she saved me that I might get something, but since she didn't say I'd see dead people, then I didn't go back to her. Could this be from her?" He said that all he knew was that she'd been shot in the head by her father and that Brandy had given her magic. "What do I do with this?"

"Do they bother you?" She said the ghosts were all right, but seeing them wasn't. "I'm assuming that they look like they're dead."

"What?" He shook his head and told her that he was trying. "I know. Right now, there is a woman standing next to you, and she wants me to tell you thanks. I didn't ask her for what because I've not spoken to any of them, but she said that you helped her."

"But you can hear them?" She nodded, and when her sister joined her in the room, she felt better. The connection between the two of them had gotten stronger since she had left her home for the last time, and she wanted her nearby all the time. "Do you suppose they have questions too? I mean, you're not answering them, right? What do they say to you? You know I don't know what to do about this. Maybe we should tell your mother—"

"Not yet." Ayden nodded. "She'd freak out, and I'm not ready for the two of us to be freaked out. You're not yet, but I'm worried about your eye twitching like it is." She watched as he covered up his eye and smiled at her. "That's not as reassuring as you'd think right now."

"Okay. Let me make notes." She wanted to roll her eyes at him. He was forever making notes but didn't say anything to him. "You can see ghosts, and you've not spoken to any of them. All right, good. Do they ask you questions?"

"They want to know what happened to me all of the sudden. Like the bullet that Aunt Brandy saved me from." He made a note, and she nodded. Maybe this note thing was better. Harley asked her what she wanted from the ghosts. "Nothing. I mean, I don't know them, and I don't know that I want to know them."

"Are they messed up?" She had to think about what Harley was asking her and nodded when she realized that she wanted to know if they were like they had died. "Okay. That's good to know. I mean, you can look at them—the ghost you said was with Ayden? What does she look like?"

"She's all cut up. Not so she's falling apart, but she is missing her right hand." Ayden looked at her sharply. "I didn't do it."

"No, I know you didn't, sweetie. But can you please ask her if she was part of the restaurant? I think she'll understand what I mean." Selma told him that she was nodding. "She was part of the murders at the restaurant that night. The bodies that we found."

"Tell him please that I'd been missing for several weeks, and when he found us, my parents knew that I didn't run off and leave them. Him finding my body, at least most of it, gave them a story behind why I was missing." She told Ayden what the woman was saying to her. "Tell him there are others that want to thank him as well. But I was voted the least scary for you to talk to."

"Can she hear me, honey?" Selma nodded, feeling like she was finally making some progress in what was going on. "I don't know your name. I was never told any of them, but I'm so happy that I was in the right place to be able to solve your disappearance."

Selma couldn't help it. She cried when the body just faded out. It was working; no matter that he didn't understand anything more than she did, Ayden was helping her solve the mystery with the ghosts. While her sister held her hand, Ayden made notes on the people who were in the room with them. Once he had notes on the ones that she could see, she told him a little bit about the people. And they were people he told her that just needed her to help.

"But I think we need to tell your mom. This isn't a secret that I'm comfortable with keeping." She said she understood. "If you want to do it while we're all together, I'll get her and give her a heads up so she's not freaked out like you said."

Ayden left them there with a kiss on their heads. He was like that, always holding them, hugging them just when they needed it. He'd talk to their mom, and things would be all right. She didn't know why she felt that way, but she did.

"I think we should think about calling him Dad all the time. He's been better to us since we moved in than our real dad was all our life. We don't have to do it, but I'm going to think about it." Harley squeezed her hand and told her that she was smart in doing this. "I hope so. He didn't look too freaked out, did he?"

"No. He's nervous, I think. And yeah, we should call him Dad. You're right, again, on him being good to us. But he's really good to Mom, too." Harley told her that she loved her. "I really do. And as much as I love you, I'm glad that I don't have this thing. I'd be rude, and they'd be banging at my door all the time, wanting me to say I'm sorry for something that I said."

It made her laugh. Something that she'd not done since she'd been able to see the first ghost. Harley had always been the best sister in the world, and she could make her laugh more than anyone. Glad now that she had told her, she asked her what she thought of the man in the barn.

"I've been thinking about him. How he's not allowed to come into the house. I think that he might be his dad." She asked her sister why she'd think that. "You said he had a hold in his chest and that he looked nasty like he didn't bathe all the time?"

"Yeah, that's right." She thought of the man and his anger. He was really mad about Ayden all the time and wanted her to get their uncle Lica to come and see him. "I think you might be right. I know that I can make him go away, but I don't want to do that unless Ayden...Dad tells me to. He might have something to say to him."

The more she thought about it, the more she believed that Harley was right. That the man was the father of the Fraizer boys and that he had something to say to them. She knew that Dad's mom was in prison, but she didn't know what either of them looked like. Thinking about it, she was happy when her mom showed up with Ayden, and she looked all right.

"Ghosts, huh?" She nodded, her eyes filling with tears again as her mom sat on the desk in front of her. "Ayden said that you don't talk to them, but I have a feeling that you have been. The other night, you were arguing with someone in your room. Is that right?"

"He's one of the men that were killed about two weeks ago. He wants me to make him live again. I don't know that I can do that. I mean, dead is dead, right?" Mom told her that was right, but if he got mean with her, to send him away. "I can do that. I haven't yet, but I can." She looked at Dad. "Your dad is here too. Not here but in the barn. I won't let him in the house anymore."

"Did he hurt you?" She said that he screams at her all the time. "That sounds like him. You can send him away if you want. I have nothing to say to him."

"He wants to talk to Uncle Lica." He seemed to be startled by that and then nodded. "He said that you all owe him, and he wants you to kill my uncle so that he's on the other side with him. I don't think that would be a good idea. He looks mean mugged all the time."

"I'll talk to my brothers and see what they want to do. You did well in not letting him in the house. I don't know what he'd do to any of us, but you were brilliant for not letting him near us." She said that she was finding out all kinds of things dealing with the dead. "I bet you are, honey. And I'm so sorry that you're having to deal with this. If Brandy knew, she'd still save you, but she'd feel bad about it."

It was only about ten minutes later when they were all meeting in the barn. The man was still there. She and Harley had decided that they weren't going to call him grandda but just the man. Uncle Edmond asked her to ask him what he wanted.

"You tell them that they're to kill off Lica." She told him that no one was going to do that. "You little bitch, you'll do what you're told, or so help me, what I gave them boys of mine, you'll think it was a walk in the mall." She corrected him. Telling the others what he was saying.

"Why does he hate me so much? Can you ask him that, sweetie? He's had it out for me since I was born." Since the man could hear them speaking, Selma just looked at him. "Tell him too that all of can—" She told them that he could hear them and that all he had to do was to talk to them. "Good. Old man, you leave my niece alone. What do you have against me? It's not anything to do with her."

"You tell him what I tell you." She told him that she wasn't going to cuss. "You will, or I'll slap you around, too. I can do it, too."

"I'm not afraid of you. And if you don't want me to send you away, you'll be nice to me or else. I won't cuss. My momma raised me better than that, and Dad here, he's the best person in the world for taking care of me and my sister. My mom is happy, too."

"Old man?" The ghost looked at Lica, and she could almost feel his hate coming from him. "You never knew this, but the six of us could shift. We played you like a fiddle, and you never knew." The ghost lunged at Lica, and he must have felt something because he laughed. "Still have nothing, do you? I'm so happy that you're dead and gone." Uncle Lica looked at her. "You can send him on or whatever you need to do, honey. There isn't a thing that I can say to him that would make any of us feel any better other than to tell him that we've been able to shift since we were eight years old."

"You tell that bastard that he's to die right now." She stared at the man who had six of the most well-respected and loved men around.

Looking at her uncles and her new dad and all she could think about was that she was safe from men like him thanks to her mom having Dad in her life. "Did you hear me little shit? Tell him that I want him to pull out a gun and blow his brains out so I can talk to him over here."

"No." He sputtered for a bit, then told her that he was going to make her life a living hell. "No, you won't. And you know why? On account of you not scaring me. Not one bit." She looked at her family, all of them. "I bid you gone from here, never to return."

It sounded like he'd been sucked into a tube and spit out the other end when he disappeared. Looking at her family again, she told them that he was gone and he'd not be back. It was Brandy that told her that she was sorry for giving her this magic.

"It's all right. It wasn't before, but it is now." Taking her sister's hand, she held it tightly. "Harley and I are lucky to have you all in our family, and we're safe from people like him. Dead or alive. They can't hurt us now."

Selma felt relief. Not in that she was free of the ghosts, they were still hanging around, but because she didn't have to keep it to herself anymore. Not only that, but none of them freaked out and talked to her like it was no big deal in being able to see them. Once they were in the house again, it was cold outside, so she went to her room. It was time she wanted to get things working instead of being afraid all the time.

"I told them." The elderly man nodded and told her that she'd done good. "I don't understand why they'd not want to know you're around. I'd think that they'd be happy to know that you're here to help them. I think that Grannie Frazier would be."

"She would be, but I'm not at a point where I can talk to her yet." She nodded, not understanding but doing as asked. "You're a good girl, and I don't mind a bit in helping you with this. But as I said, I'm not ready to let them know that I'm around."

"He murdered you, didn't he?" Selma watched as he nodded slowly. "You don't have to worry about him anymore. He won't bother them or you."

"I know that." He looked at the door to her room, and she asked if he wanted her to open it. "No. Not just yet. That sister of yours is coming, and you tell her that no one will think any less of her because she's not able to see me. They'll love you both equally."

"I know that." He nodded, and his eyes widened when Grannie Fraizer came into the room. "She knows you're around, Grandda Frazier. I didn't tell her, but she knows. She told me once last week that she could feel your loving arms when she's having a rough day."

"Oh, Brogan." She helped them in a way that only she could. When they spoke to each other, as if they could hear, she left the room. While she was sure that they'd be all right, Selma knew too that Grannie Frazier wouldn't join her husband until she was nineteen. That was something else she could do, tell when someone was going to die.

~*~

Summer was so happy to have their own place. The tree in the living room was the first thing that they'd put together. It wasn't a real one, not this year, but she was about as happy with it as she'd been with anything else in the house. Even the girls were happy to have the beautifully lit tree up so soon after moving in.

Having money this year made her feel

better about spending so much on the girls. They both had their own room, and they had kept it nice, even with all the other things going on, and she wanted to reward them. She might not be able to afford to splurge next year or the years after, but this year, she was going to go all out. They were a family, and she couldn't have loved them anymore. Especially Ayden.

He'd taken to being a partner to her with all that he was. Once the girls started calling him Dad, they seemed to do it with gusto. She couldn't have been more proud of them either. She had a family now, and there wasn't anything going to come between her and hers. Not even the Fortrights were trouble anymore.

"I have a package coming in the next several days. Well, a lot of packages are coming, but don't open them. I've been having fun." She knew that it was for her, just the way that Ayden had said for her not to open it. Once she told him that she'd not, he kissed her on the mouth and moved to his office. That was another thing that she wanted for Christmas, sex with her husband.

Going into the office, she was surprised to see how organized it had been. Having only just moved into the house the week before, it looked like they'd been living there forever. Ayden was still working, so he'd had to set things up quickly, but she'd been lazing around the house, enjoying being a mom for a change, and now it was time for her to be a wife with all that it entailed. She also had to tell Ayden that she loved him. Because she did, with all her heart.

"The girls are with your grandma. She's taking them shopping for the two of us. Is that normal?" Ayden laughed and asked her if she'd just ask him if something was normal. "I guess you're right. Nothing has been normal since I met you."

"Tomorrow, there is a school function, but for the life of me, I can't remember what it is. Is that when the girls go to the school to figure out what grade they're going to be in?" She told him that it was also the Christmas pageant as well. "Oh. Yeah, I did forget about that. They're not in the pageant, are they?"

"Yes, but they don't have any parts in the play. I think they arrived too late for them to be able to get one." She sat on the chair across from Ayden. "I just heard from Brandy. She wants to go to Easton to spend the day with the kids. I don't know if I'd wander that far from home with her being as big as she is. She's not even due for another month yet."

"The doctor told her that she'd be fine so long as she didn't overdo it. I'm thinking that she's had this date with you guys planned before you became a part of the family. She told me that once, that she couldn't wait for us to have mates so that she could have friends. I've been told, and I don't know whether to believe it or not, she's not any good at making female friends." She told him that she thought she was great. "I guess most women are intimidated around her. She does have a tendency to be a little pushy."

"Only a little?" They both laughed, and she slipped out of her shoes. "I've been thinking about things with us. I know that we're married and all, but we've never really talked about what that meant." Ayden shut off his computer and asked her if she wanted to talk now. "Yes. Do you want other children than the girls? Do you mind that I'm not working but staying here all the time? Just questions that have been going through my head. Also, would you like to have sex with me?"

"Yes. I would love to have other children with you. So long as you're all right with it. Yes, I love having you home all the time because it makes you happy. And more than anything, I'd love to make love with you. Not just sex, but making love." He leaned back in the chair that he'd picked up new today. "Is this why the girls are spending the day with my grandma? Because you wanted to make love?"

"I didn't think of that when she called here for them, no. But I've been thinking about how much I love you, and it seemed natural that we have sex. Or make love as you said." She didn't move from the chair when he put his computer on the floor. "What are you doing? You're not working more, are you?"

"No. Come here so that I can taste you." She nearly fell out of the chair. "All I've thought about all month is what you might taste like. Eating you here on my desk sounds so good to me that I can barely think of anything else. Would you like that?"

"Yes." Her voice sounded husky, and she stood up only to sit back down. "There are people in the house. What if they hear us?"

"They won't." He was so sure that she believed him. Going toward him, she sat on the desk, just realizing why he'd put his computer on the floor. Putting her feet on either side of his chair arms, she leaned back on the desk. "Can you see how hard I am? It's all for you."

He didn't open his zipper, but she had no trouble seeing how hard he was. Even as he sat there, adjusting his cock, all she could feel was need. Even when her pussy felt wet, she knew that this was going to be more than she could have hoped for in making love with this man.

She moved her feet over him even as he took her hand and rubbed it against his shaft. Wrapping her fingers around him as he'd done and squeezed him. He jumped in her hand. When his free hand moved behind her neck and brought her close, she moaned again when she felt his mouth nip at her neck.

"Strip. Take your clothes off and let me taste you. Christ, I want to fuck you with my tongue." His hands were everywhere, and her clothes were torn from her even as she felt his mouth on her breasts. "Feed me, Summer. Feed me your nipples while I fuck your hand."

When her breast was free, she lifted it up to his mouth, and his teeth sank deep into her nipple, making her cry out. When he turned her around and sat her on the desk, she whimpered when he freed his cock from her hand. But his fingers slid into her pussy made her forget everything but what he was doing to her.

"I'm going to eat you, suck your pussy until you come in my mouth. Then I'm going to lap every bit of your cum in my mouth, making you come and come again."

"Please, Ayden. Please." When he got down onto his knees and pulled her ass forward until her pussy was right on the edge, she watched his head lower to her. "Ayden, Please, I—"

His tongue entered her. She felt it move inside of her. In and out, in and out. When he licked her clit she threw back her head and, using her hands, she lifted up to get him deeper. She wrapped her fingers in his hair and tried to guide him to her clit again, but he wouldn't go. Frustration was making her needy, and she wanted him to make her come with him in the worst sort of way.

When he finally took her clit into his mouth and sucked her hard, she screamed out her release.

His fingers entered her, and again, he touched off another climax, then another. She lay back when he stood, his cock thick and hard before her. There was so much precum on him that she was sure that there was going to be very little left for herself.

"Watch me. Watch what I want to do when I come inside of you." His hand fisted his cock and stroked it once twice, then a third time before he came. "Oh baby, yes."

Thick hot cum jettisoned out from him and onto her belly, breasts, and face. He roared with each release, and when he reached down and pinched her clit she came again, screaming out his name as he rubbed his cum all over her.

He wasted no time in taking her this time. His cock filled her to her throat, it felt like, and she wanted to feel his cum. Rubbing his juices all over her, she nearly fainted when her hands rubbed his cum on her breasts. All she could think of as he filled her was that she was never going to be the same again.

"I'm coming." She fell back on the desk, her body tight with anticipation. As soon as he bit down on her shoulder, she came so hard that she thought that she was broken. Even as she came a second, then a third time, she knew that, on some level, this wasn't normal. This wasn't the way that people made love. When he growled at her, his voice in her head, she came again when ordered and passed out.

When she woke, she was on his lap—it had to have been only a few seconds. His cock was deep inside of her. Almost as soon as she sat up, feeding him her breasts, she threw back her head and came again.

Nothing could have prepared her for having this kind of love, and when he pulled her to him, her clit at his groin, Summer screamed out his name and let herself tumble over into the bliss that was theirs and theirs alone.

This time, when she woke up, she was still in his arms, but her body was lying across his. He wasn't talking, but she could tell that he was deep in thought. Sitting up a bit more, he smiled at her as he adjusted her on his lap.

"I love you." His grin got bigger, and she told him that she loved him as well. "I want to prepare you for the magic—" But it was too late. It was rolling over her like a thunderstorm in the middle of summer.

Her body felt turned inside out. Fingers cramping up, it was all she could do to hold onto him. While he held onto her, Summer could feel her feet tightening. Her hair seemed to crackle in her mind. Even as she held onto him, Ayden kept saying that he was sorry that he had her and that she'd be all right. Passing blissfully out, she knew that this wasn't finished, but she couldn't take the pain any longer.

Looking around the room, she knew that she was in her bed. The room wasn't dark, but just enough that she had to squint to see what was in the room with her. It was Ayden who spoke to her, seemingly from a long distance and told her that she was all right that it was over. Closing her eyes, she knew that if it was over, she was going to have magic that would only be revealed by Brandy and Mac. Her body was just too sore to care if she could even see ghosts like her daughter.

Getting out of bed and going to the bathroom, she didn't make a sound as she made her way across the room. The bottom of her feet hurt, and she thought that she would have a permanent cramp in her hands as she made her way back to the bed. When Ayden lifted the covers, she got into bed with him and snuggled closer to him. The walk to the bathroom had been chilly, but she was warmer now that she had Ayden at her side.

The sun was up when she got out of bed again. There were damp towels hanging on the rack and smallish footprints on the floor from water dripping. Taking a shower and letting the too-hot water run over her, she began to feel better even as she stretched out. Her only thought was that if they made love like that again, she was going to be too sore to move. Hopefully, it was something that didn't happen every day. Then she realized that she did want that every day and smiled. She didn't know what to think when she found herself with the ability to dress herself with magic.

Chapter 4

The house was full of items that they knew would be in great demand. Guy loved being able to help, and when it was his turn to do inventory, he didn't mind having to be inside at all. In fact, he thought that he could do this forever. Picking up the house phone when it rang, he answered with "Fraizer" Not giving much away as to what he was doing there. Whoever it was, they were going to be shocked that he was in such a great mood. Because he was, damn it.

"Tell me how many diapers I can have? And I want full boxes too, not you bundling them up in a bag for me." He didn't recognize the voice, so he said his name again. "I don't care who this is. If you're going to be giving away shit, I want some of it. How many diapers can I have?"

"I'm sorry, but I don't know what you're talking about. How did you get this number? In order to qualify, you have to fill out an application before you get anything from the charity." She let out a string of curse words that frankly embarrassed him. "We don't sell diapers. And unless you have applied for them, I can't help you. This is a charity, not a store."

"I'm not going to pay for them, dumbass. The lady that works for me — well, she used to work for me said that she got free shit from you guys, and I want some of it." He asked her again if she'd filled out an application. "No, and I'm not going to fill one out either. Why should I have to pay for them when you're out there giving shit away just because someone popped out a kid that they can't afford. I'm betting my taxes pay for this anyway, and I want my fair share."

"This is a charity that works with donations. We have nothing to do with the government." She told him bullshit. "Well, it's been nice talking to you, but as I said, I'm not going to give you anything until it's been approved."

"Listen here, you mother fucker, you're going to do what I tell you because of who I... do you have any idea who you're talking to? I'm going to own that little business you have gone by the end of the day if you don't do what I want. I'm a woman who gets what she wants no matter what the application is. Mother fuck. It's just diapers. Give me enough to get me by for the year, and I'll not have to sue you."

"And what do you think you'd be suing me for? Not giving a person diapers when you can obviously afford them? No, I don't think so." He put the phone back on the shelf after disconnecting the call and continued with his inventory. When it rang again, he simply ignored it.

He was nearly done when he noticed that there were several messages on the answering machine. As he listened to the woman, her getting angrier and angrier each time he didn't answer, he laughed his ass off as he made his way to his car. Glad that he'd started it before he'd come out— it was freezing outside. Something hit him from behind, and Guy hit the ground.

Waking up, he realized two things at once. He was in the hospital, and his brothers were all in the room with him. Asking them what happened, it was Ayden who answered him after telling them that they had it on record that his head was harder than anyone else.

"I suppose that is supposed to make sense."

They laughed, and he realized that he did have a major headache. "Some woman did this. I remember just before I fell out of it that I could smell perfume."

"Mrs. Hathaway. She's the mayor's wife. I'm so glad that we put up the security cameras before we opened. She was there to knock you out, too, as she had a ball bat." He asked why she'd done that to him. "Don't know. She didn't say anything other than hitting you. There were several missed calls from her in the building, but none of them made any sense to us."

"I remember now. She wanted diapers. Boxes of them." He explained what had transpired between the two of them while he'd been doing inventory. "She said that if we were giving them away, then she should have some too. Something about suing us as well, but I don't remember that too much."

"We're not a profit place. Suing us would be like suing the road." Ayden told him that he was going to have to have x-rays before they'd let him home. "As it is now, you need about a dozen stitches. And she's been arrested because Capshaw said that had you been human, she would have killed you, so he's charging her with attempted murder."

"She was saying that we gave some to someone that worked for her. I didn't get a name, but since we've only helped about half a dozen people, and only one of them is getting diapers, I think we can narrow it down a bit." Ayden said that was what they thought as well after listening to the messages. "I ignored her after the first call. After that, I finished up and went out to my car only to be hit by her."

"That's what the cameras showed, too." The nurse came in and asked him if he wanted anything for pain, and he told her yes. Talking to his brothers was making him realize how bad his head was hurting. "They're going to keep you overnight so that they can keep an eye on you, but I'll come and get you in the morning. All right?"

"Yes, that's good. Do I have to press charges?" It was Ivan who told him that he'd have to get with the police when he was home to do that, but since she'd hurt him, Caroline was going to be spending the night in jail. And that her husband was none too thrilled that they were jailing her. "Too bad. She's off her noodle. I didn't even know that they had little kids that needed diapers."

"They don't. She was telling the police that she was going to resell them and that someone should be making some money off of what we were doing. People are crazier all the time if you ask me." Everyone agreed with his brother, and he asked for something to eat. "They don't want you to eat either, buddy. Sorry. But like I said, I'd pick you up in the morning, and then I'll make sure you have plenty to eat before I take you back to my house. The girls want to pamper you because you were so brave."

He made it sound as if he didn't think it was so brave, but he didn't care. The meds were kicking in, and he was feeling better by the minute. Closing his eyes, he realized that the light was bothering him, and he just wanted them all to go away. It was too much for him to listen to them making fun of him for being hit by a girl.

Waking in the middle of the night, he tried to figure out what time it was on his phone. His eyesight was blurry, and he was a little sick to his stomach. Finding the nurse call button, he had to calm himself when he started begging for help. He needed more for the pain, and he wanted them to bring him something that he could throw up in. Christ, he really was sick.

The next time he woke up, Ayden was in the chair beside the bed. Saying his name, he was startled by the worried look on his face. Telling him what had happened when the nurse came in, he was glad now that he'd spent the night in the hospital instead of being at home with Ayden and his daughters.

"They said you called out for them, then passed out, puking in the bed." He told his brother that he'd not remembered that. "Yeah, I kinda got that feeling too. Anyway, they were worried and did another x-ray of your noodle and found a small crack in your skull. The doctors said that had you been home, you might well have died because of how much you were throwing up without being conscious. Christ, you scared the hell out of all of us."

It scared him, too, and he wondered if he could have anything for pain now. He was told that he could have whatever he wanted so long as he didn't get sick again. Closing his eyes again when the meds kicked in, Guy was thrilled when his brother took his hand into his. It was something that he'd not felt in decades, the thought of being alone and someone trying to hurt him.

It was late afternoon when his brothers showed up again. This time, there wasn't any joking around, only concern that he'd been so sick. He was teary-eyed when the girls had made him a card with glitter all over it and had to take a few deep breaths when they told him that they loved him. Christ, he loved his family.

Being on clear liquids didn't bother him as much as he thought it would. He wasn't really all that hungry, but he was glad for the things that came with his diet. Selma, he knew that she'd seen ghosts, was telling him about a man that she'd been helping, and then Harley told him about the presents she'd been putting under the tree.

"There are so many under the tree, Uncle Guy, that we look like one of those Christmas commercials on television. Mom didn't have the money to get us very much when she was working all the time, so it's really neat to see them there. One of them has your name on it." He asked her if she'd shake it for him. "Nah, you'll have to wait like the rest of us do. But I know that it's bigger than Uncle Lica's."

That made him laugh. As he was resting, something that he thought he wasn't all that good at, he got some more information on Caroline. The woman had been terrorizing her employees for weeks, and the police were about ready to send her home she was cursing so much.

"She's not normally like this, I guess." Guy asked Devlin what he meant. "Nothing. I mean, she's usually this cool and collected type of woman, and in the last few weeks, she's been off the rail. I suggested that there was something wrong with her, and I got made fun of. But humans don't just change their ways like that overnight."

"Did you tell the doctor?" He said that he mentioned it, but no one was taking him seriously. "I'd make them listen to you. She might have something really wrong with her, and you know how humans can be."

When the doctor came in, Devlin told them about the woman and what he'd heard about her changing her behavior. The man wasn't listening, telling him that it would be up to her family to see what was going on. It wasn't until Lica told the man that he needed to listen before he took them at their word. This just didn't sound right.

It was nearly midnight when he heard from the staff that Mrs. Hathaway had suffered a stroke and had died. It hurt his heart to know that she might well have been saved if someone had listened to her earlier when she told her own doctor that she wasn't feeling right. According to the staff, she'd been coming out of the store a few weeks ago when she'd had an episode. Telling them that she didn't feel right, whatever that meant to the woman, she was sent on her way home with a pat on her head. She'd been getting sicker as the weeks went on, and by the time that someone had listened to her, it had been too late to save her. Guy almost felt sorry for her husband, but he should have listened to her as well. The poor woman.

"They said that she'd been in the hospital several times in the last few days. She complained of chest pains, headaches, and dizziness. Since they didn't find anything on the EKG they ran, they sent her home with some pain pills and even had the nerve to tease her a little about coming into the emergency department so many times when she'd not been coming in before." Guy asked if there was going to be a lawsuit. "More than likely, but we won't hear anything about it for a while. Mr. Hathaway is trying to get his house in order because of her being arrested when you wouldn't have been hurt either had someone done something sooner."

He was going to stay out of it. There was enough going around that he'd not have to get involved about it with humans. Guy didn't care all that much for humans anyway. His sisters-in-law were all right, but he didn't find himself hanging around them all that much.

"I have a question for you." He smiled when he thought of Brandy getting in touch with him. *"You told me when you were doing the inventory the last time that things weren't getting used fast enough. Did you mean everything or just the water that you reported?"*

"What else was in there that would have expired?" She told him. *"I didn't think about that. But what kind of best if bought by date would water have if they're not being used."*

"I don't know. But if they do and we use them beyond that point, are we going to be in trouble if something happens?" He told her again that he didn't know. *"I don't either. I'm going to get with an attorney to see what I can find out. We'll only buy them*

if we need them if it's going to be a problem."

"There are other things that we need to talk about. Like there should be people at the building at all times. It might not be a big deal with us starting out, but I'm fearful for anyone who wants to come around again, and someone might be hurt. There is no telling how long I would have been out there without the cameras." Brandy said she'd not thought of that. *"I've been thinking about a great many things since I was hurt. Like I think that we need to have security out there all the time. It might save us a bit of trouble in the long run. People will get into their heads that they can come out at any time and cause trouble."*

"You might be right about that. I'm not used to people wanting to get into my stuff. It's not like I had any before you guys came along." He told her that he was sorry. *"Don't be. You've made me a better person, and I love you guys."*

It took him another hour to figure out when he was going to go home. He wasn't keen on the idea of staying with his brother, but he knew too that he'd been lucky to have been here where people could watch him, and he didn't want that to happen again. He found that he was nervous about a lot of things of late.

He didn't mind being alone, but not for long periods of time. He didn't enjoy going out to eat on his own, but he would do it so that he'd not be afraid all the time. Guy needed to get his shit together so that he wasn't going to be a recluse like his grandpa had become in his later years.

~*~

Ayden looked over the paperwork that Brandy had given him about the charity house. He didn't know what they were going to call it yet, but he sort of liked Charity House. As the contract was going to have someone there all the time, he wondered at the idea of having someone living in the house that they used so that if there was an emergency, they could get things gathered up before the person or persons came around and that would be one less thing that they had to worry about.

"There are seven pallets of water that have a best by date on them of next year. If we don't use them all by then, then I think we need to rethink having water around all the time for emergencies." He asked Summer what sort of things they might use the water for. "I was thinking about that too, and I've come up with a couple of ideas. They're not mine, but things that I've seen on the news. A house fire comes to mind. To have for the victims and the firefighters."

"Yes, that would be better than using them to put the fire out." She laughed with him. "I've spoken to a couple of people about living in the place. I don't know that we'd want just anyone in there. I have this feeling that they'd be giving shit away to their friends. I'm not very trusting nowadays. Not since Guy was hurt."

"I find myself looking at people like I'm waiting for them to pull out a gun. I don't care for feeling that way." He said that he didn't either. "By the way, the mayor is suing the hospital and the staff. I think he's going to win, but I don't know. Can you sue a hospital? I'm going to look it up."

"I don't know that either. I know that you can sue doctors for malpractice or negligence if they do something wrong. And I think you can sue surgeons, too. But I'd have to have a look into it. Are you planning something?" She laughed and told him that with Brandy having a baby, she's worried about everything lately. "I guess I can understand that. Guy has never been trusting. When he was a kid, he was taken advantage of by some humans. That's what he calls them, humans.

And he's never been trusting of them since. I don't remember the details, but I remember Dad and Mom both beating him nearly to death when he was caught."

"I think from what I heard, your parents beat all of you like that." That was true, but he didn't like to think about that right now. "Selma is coming to see you. She has a dad question. Are you all right with them calling you dad?"

"Are you kidding? It's the best thing ever. I love it when she calls my brothers uncles, too. It's like they were born into this family, and we've been together forever." She laughed a little with him. "I get a wife and two daughters right off the bat. What man wouldn't be happy about that?"

"I guess I never thought about it as you having a family. They've been mine since…well, for all their lives. But having you in our lives has made so many changes. They do sleep better, and I know that I do as well. It's nice having a home to go to and not to mention an entire family to depend on, too." He said that he loves that as well. "Oh, I have to go. I have some things that I have to take care of right now."

After she left him to do her thing, he opened

his computer to look at the investments that he'd been playing with. He'd not ever been one to take chances with his money—not that he'd had all that much, but he did want to make sure that if Summer wanted to be a stay-at-home mom, he could still provide them with the things that they needed.

It was nearly an hour later when he finished up with Selma. She'd been having some issues at the new school and wanted to talk to him about them. She told him that her mom would have gone in with guns blazing to take care of it, but all she'd wanted was for him to advise her on what to do. Not solve it for her.

"If he's giving you a hard time, just talk to him." She said that she'd tried that, but he was so rude. "Boys are like that. When they like someone, they have to show off. I never did. I was too afraid of women to even talk to them very much. Teasing them would have given me a heart attack."

The two of them laughed, and she sat down in the chair across from him. He was never sure what was going to come out of Selma's mouth. Harley was easier to read and more fun to be around, but with Selma, he felt as if he needed to be on his best behavior. Sometimes, he was actually afraid of her. When she looked at him, he decided that he was going to get to know her better. Even if she did frighten him a bit, he needed to know her as well as he did her sister and mother.

"I'm not sure what I want to be when I grow up. I'm afraid that the ghosts will have a lot to do with how I get a job and stuff." He asked her if she'd been thinking about what she wanted to be when she got older. "You know what mom would have said? She would have told me that I had plenty of time to figure that out and I didn't need to worry myself. Thank you for that."

"You're so very welcome. But what is it that you'd like to do? I'm sure that you do have plenty of time, but it's nice to know what you have to do to get there. Like what sort of education you might need to work on. And now that you're in third grade, that means that you're nearly halfway finished with your high school. You know what, you don't have a lot of time." He laughed again, and it felt good to be able to do that. "Selma, I'm going to make sure that you and your sister have a good education. And that you won't have to work during college if I can manage it. Brandy said something about setting up a fund for the kids that come along, but since I've not talked to her about it, I don't know what the requirements will be."

"She'll probably...I was going to say that it would be only for kids that were born of this family but she'd not do that. She'd think of us all as being born into the Frazier family." He said he thought that she was correct in that. "I think so as well. Anyway, I'm going to apply for some grants and scholarships, too. And I'm going to keep my grades up so that I can win some money that way, too. It would be smarter for me to know that I can get into any college I want because I'm smart, not because I have the money to get in. Does that make sense?"

"It does, actually." Closing up his computer, he devoted his time to her and the conversation that they were having. By the time dinner was called, not only had he found out that she was a good deal smarter than he was, but that she was compassionate as well. He loved her. He had always loved her, but today helped him get to know her better, and that felt good.

After dinner of sloppy joes and tater tots, he was ready to call it a day. The girls had to clean up the kitchen since he and Summer had cooked, and he loved the way that the two of them seemed to know on some level that they had to give as good as they got.

Ayden loved that Summer hadn't asked about what they'd talked about. Even though Selma had told her most of it, she never badgered him into talking her into anything. He supposed all families were like that, but since he didn't know, he was learning as he went.

The snow was coming down pretty hard when he was locking up the house. He figured that the kids wouldn't have school tomorrow due to the roads being covered and was happy to be able to spend the day with them. Summer had a luncheon with Brandy at the main house, and since it wasn't canceled, he was glad when she said that she was going to walk there rather than drive. He had more paperwork to fill out and file, so his day was going to be at home anyway. Just as he was headed up to bed, he heard from Guy.

"They're releasing me tomorrow. Can I stay with you?" Ayden told him that he would enjoy that. *"I can't be alone until I don't have a headache anymore. It's better, don't get me wrong, but I'd rather not have a sick episode like I did before."*

"I don't want you to either. I was just thinking that the girls won't have school tomorrow, so they'll be home to be around you. Take advantage of them, please. They've been looking forward to pampering you for the last few days." Guy said that he didn't know how much he could take of that. *"Just don't hurt their feelings by yelling at them to go away. All right? I'd hate to have to send you back to the hospital for making my daughters cry."*

"I won't, I promise." They talked about the things that he was going to be doing when he was better. *"I've been looking at houses since I've been in here. I can't look all that long, but I know enough about houses to kind of have an idea of what I want. I don't want fucking huge, but I would like something with a few bedrooms in it. When the kids come along, I'm going to be the uncle that they stay with for fun."*

"You'll need to have a big house simply because if you're the fun uncle, they'll be wanting to stay a lot more." He told him that he could live with that. *"Good. Aren't you planning to have a mate, Guy? I mean, it's in the cards, I think what with the three of us having one so far."*

"I don't want a mate. I mean, if she comes along, then great, but otherwise, I'm not going to go out

looking for her. I don't have my life set right now, and I don't see that happening anytime soon. I'm just loving the way that I can come and go as I please and not have to worry about anyone else." He paused, but before he could say anything, he continued. *"I don't have my life in any kind of order. I'm twenty-five years old, and I'm just now getting to the point where I think I can live with myself. I don't have any kind of furniture, no good memories from when I was a kid — none of us do, and I've gotten to the point in my life where I want people to just leave me alone, not family, and let me do my own thing."*

"You sound set in your ways if you ask me. Don't be that guy who yells at kids for being on his lawn after he mows it. Nor the person with a hundred dogs around. You're better than that." He laughed which what he was going for. *"I'll come and get you in the morning. If there is any change let me know. As I said, the girls will be off school, I'm betting, and Brandy and the other women have some things to take care of. Also, you can help me think of something to get the people of my house for Christmas."*

"Money." He had been thinking the same thing but didn't like that money was just all he could think of, but he knew that a lot of people struggled

this time of year. Going into the bedroom that he shared with Summer, he was disappointed that she was asleep already. He'd wanted to snuggle and with her asleep, she'd kick him to the side if she was comfy already.

Waking once in the middle of the night, he was surprised to see that Summer was already up. She'd gotten a text from the school saying that the girls would be off, and he was all right with being home with them. After telling her about Guy, she rolled over toward him and wrapped her now cold body around his. Almost before he could tell her that she was too cold, she was sleeping. He wished he could fall asleep that easily.

It took him until nearly midnight to get his mind to slow down enough that he could relax. Every time he would close his eyes, he'd think of something new, and he'd be off again. Before the sun came up, he finally closed his eyes. Since he didn't have to get up too early, he was going to sleep as late as his brother would allow him to.

It was nearly noon when he heard from his brother. Getting out of the shower, he was dressed and at the hospital at one. The roads had been taken care of, and it wasn't that bad. He was glad, too, that he'd had the girls stay home. He was stressed enough by the time he got his brother and was home again that he needed another nap. Things were working out well for the household, and he was having a good time being the one who could take care of his little brother.

Chapter 5

Donna hid as best she could in the trash area in the back of the restaurant. She'd been hiding out for days now, and she was no closer to being out of town than she'd been all those weeks ago. Having an abusive husband wasn't what she wanted in life. In fact, what she wanted was someone to love her and to take care of her needs. Instead of her taking care of everyone else's needs.

Hearing the man from the place bringing out the trash for the night, she stayed as still as she could. He'd been good to her so far, bringing her out food that he'd made rather than her having to dig around in the trash. When he lit a cigarette, she waited for him to speak. He did this nightly, telling her what he'd brought her to eat.

"There is a phone number that I left you in the bag. There is a phone too, as you said you didn't have one." She watched him, barely breathing so she'd not miss what he was saying. "There is a place too that you can get help. It's all on the paper that I put there for you. A man came in looking for you today, and nobody said where you were."

Someone other than him knew that she was around? It made her sick to think that she might well end up back at Donnie's house. The man was a terror to her, and she didn't want to ever have to be back in that house again.

When they married three years ago, she thought him the best person in the world. He'd had a good job and a nice car, and he even had a couple of credit cards that he'd given her to use for groceries and stuff. Her job of being a dental assistant had dried up when the doctor she'd been working for was charged with sexual deviancy. He'd not bothered her, but she did read in the paper that he'd been fondling little kids when he'd put them under for teeth being pulled. She'd also heard that he had done the same thing to other men, and she was glad to be out of there. Then Donnie lost his job.

Things had been all right for a little while. They'd had a savings account that had held them over until one of them got another job. But then she began hearing things about Donnie and what he had been caught doing on the job. The man had been selling drugs to kids around the neighborhood.

Once he'd been arrested, never believing that he'd do such a thing, she stood beside her man while she waited tables in the local pizza joint. Then, one night, out of the blue, he'd knocked her around when she'd come home with fewer tips than she had the night before. It had taken her nearly a week to be able to go back to her job, where everyone warned her that Donnie had a temper and she might be better off leaving him.

It was the first time that he'd hit her, and she didn't want to make a snap judgement about him for that. There had been a great deal of stress in the household, and he was having trouble getting even a first interview for another job. When he did start to work, the man at the gas station had hired him until he found out that the rumors were true, that Donnie had been selling the drugs to the kids, and that he hadn't stopped.

It nearly cost her life when she asked him about it. As it was now, she was having trouble seeing out of one eye and had a hearing problem with certain high-pitched sounds. As soon as she was out of the hospital, she packed up her things while he was in jail and left. That had been three months ago, and he'd brought her back twice now and beaten her again.

She needed to get away, and the only way that she knew how to do it was to depend on others. But the issue with that was that they all believed him when he told them that she was a part of the drugs being sold as well.

"Also, I've spoken to Mr. Fraizer. He's the one that is running the charity place. He said to tell you that if you want out of town, all you need to do is meet him at the place at midnight tonight, and he'll make sure you can have enough to start over." She wanted to ask him if he trusted him, but she couldn't speak. Fear made her mute when she needed answers, and she was out in the open like she was right now. "He said that you'd be safe if you came around as his brothers were there as well. You know that they're wolves, right?"

Again, she didn't answer him. It was bad enough that all she had for company was herself, but talking to a stranger that she didn't even know his name was terrible, too. Wiping at the tears that had done her no good so far, she said 'yes' to his queries for the first time since she'd been hiding out.

It was nearly eleven when she made her way to the charity place. It was well-lit, something else that she was afraid of, and there didn't seem to be anyone around. As she was staying to the edges of the house, she heard a low growl and looked in the direction she thought it had come from.

There standing there was a great gray wolf. He lay down when she leapt back against the building, but he didn't say anything. It wasn't until someone, another man, came out of the darkness that she felt like she might be able to make it. He told her his name was Ayden, and the wolf with him was his brother Guy.

"We have a ticket for you for the bus station. There are some things too that you can put on so that no one recognizes you." She took the bag that he told her was beside her. "I'll take you to the station, not the one here in town but across the county, and help you get on it. The ticket is for a round trip to the furthest end of the line, but you get off at Pillsbury Station. Once there, there will be someone there that will meet you and get you further downstate."

"I don't have any identification." He said that it was taken care of and that no one would know she was on the bus so long as she didn't cause trouble. "I won't. I promise you."

After getting all the instructions that she was going to need, a big car pulled up, and she was asked to get into it. That was something that she'd only just realized. No one had ordered her to do anything but had been polite in asking her to do what was needed.

By the time the car pulled out of the lot, she was dressed in baggy clothing, a wig on her head, and a nice warm coat that she'd missed having. Getting her food situated in her new 'purse,' she was ready to go when the car pulled up in front of the station house. Christ, she was terrified, but so far things had gone—

"Don't move." She didn't even blink or breathe when the man stopped in front of her. "Your husband is over there, see him?"

She whimpered when she saw him and the man told her that he had her. Ayden assured her that he'd not get to her, and Guy took off as his wolf again to chase him away. It might well have been funny, but she was terrified out of her mind.

Getting on the bus an hour later, she had a newspaper to read, several puzzle books as well as another change of clothing. Donna had lost so much weight that she was afraid that a good wind would blow her over, but for the first time in months, she felt like she might be able to survive her leaving her husband.

The bus seemed to be traveling forever. It was warm on the thing, and she found herself dozing a bit off and on. The big man, the wolf Guy, had followed her onto the bus, but he didn't sit with her. As she became more sleepy and more exhausted, she found herself feeling safe for the longest time.

When the bus pulled into the Pillsbury Station, she waited until everyone got off before she did. Guy got off after she did and when she went into the station house, there was a note on her luggage. There was another hundred dollars for her to take a hotel room in the name of Brandy Fraizer, and she was to meet up with someone in the morning who would take her the rest of the way.

Nerves got the better of her, and she sat in the hotel room, waiting for someone to break the door down and come after her. She wanted a bath and a soak in a tub but was afraid of that as well. Everything seemed to scare the shit out of her. When the phone beside her chirped, she nearly had herself a heart attack before she could answer it.

"It's Guy. I'm going to take you to dinner. I have your husband's scent now, so he's not around. Meet me in the dining room." She told him that he didn't have to do that. "I don't have to do a lot of things, but I want to do this. You need some normal in your life, and I'm going to give it to you the best that I can. Also, I have pictures of the people that you're meeting tomorrow, and I thought that would be easier on you."

She met him there and was glad when he made it seem like it was old friends having a meal. It was the first one that she'd had in a while, and she was determined to enjoy every minute of it.

By the time he was walking her to her door, the burger and fries being divine, telling her that she'd be all right, not only did she have pictures of the people who were going to help her, but he'd given her two credit cards that she could use with her name on them. Also, an identification card with a picture that looked enough like her that it would pass as being her.

Taking a bath, she felt like a new person. Her body was clean, and her hair was soft. Everything about this was going to get her out of harm's way. As soon as she lay down on the bed, the hotel was going to call her when she was to get up. Donna fell into a deep sleep and didn't wake up once, not even to go to the bathroom.

The people met her in the dining room again and hugged her like they were old friends. She enjoyed their company and was glad that they didn't mention her leaving. It was a short visit with them, and she was happy for the friendship that they were making.

"I'm to tell you that your husband is in jail. He's going to be there for the next couple of days, for as long as they can hold him for breaking and entering. You'll be settled into your own home by then and starting your new job." She said that she didn't have any experience at anything just yet. "You'll be fine. Also, there are several numbers that you can call if you need anything, but the Fraizers are finished, all right?"

Telling them yes, she was asked what she'd

change about their involvement on the way she was getting out. It took her a few minutes to figure out anything that had been done wrong, and all she could think about and it wasn't really anything wrong, but she thought that they needed better wigs. It was all that she had for them.

"I'll let them know." The three of them laughed. "I thought you'd say something like it needed more money or something like that."

"They gave me five hundred dollars the first night and gave me a ticket to get out of town. I think it's more money than I've had in a while, and I was actually nervous about spending it. Waiting for the other shoe to drop, I guess." Peggy, the woman with the man named David, told her that they tried very hard not to have that much cash on them, so when an emergency came up, they weren't able to supply them with much. "I have enough to get food in the house, and that's all I can think about right now."

The ride to the next town was quiet. Peggy gave her advice on things that she was to do. Told her about her job and what was going to be expected of her. She wasn't to take on a job that she had before, as that would give Donnie a clue as to where she was.

By that evening, exhausted again, she was in her new place. It was furnished and had a lot of touches that made her feel like it was a real home for her so that she was comfortable by the time she was ready for bed. Someone had even put up a little tree and put gifts under it for her, but she didn't open them. Life, she decided, was going to be much better than it was now, and she was going to make sure that she didn't let things jade her, what Peggy had told her because not everyone was like her soon-to-be ex-husband.

When she got up the next day, the first day of her new life she was calling it, Donna went to her job with a new attitude on not just life but everything in her life now.

~*~

Summer was at the auction when she heard from Guy about the woman that they were helping. She'd made it to her home and had started her new job just this morning. Summer decided that she was going to pick up clothing from garage sales this summer and keep a supply of wigs and purses for women and children.

The idea had come from Mac's brothers.

They had been moving people around for years and had never once been caught at it. They didn't use wigs and such. They just picked the person up that their grandmother wanted them to kill, took them someplace else, and handed them money to get them a new start. They, however, were in a network of people that helped them, and it was working out better, she thought, with getting them as far away as they could.

"Mom, there is a ghost in the room with you." Stopping what she was doing in favor of seeing to her daughter, she asked her who it was. "I don't know. They want me to talk to you about something."

"Okay. But just so you know, I don't know all that many people that are dead." She told her that she knew that, too. As soon as Selma sat down with Harley, she had a feeling that the two of them were ganging up on her about something. "What's going on?"

"This person has been gone for a very long time. You need to know that right up front." She nodded, unsure where this was going. "He used to live here in this house, at least a part of it, a long time ago and wants you to understand that the things he left behind are for you. For helping the people that need to get away."

"Is he related to the person that we just helped?" It was Harley who answered yes. "I see. I don't really, but I'm beginning to understand. This man, whoever he is, wants us to use his, for lack of a better term, treasures to help fund the helping of people get out of bad situations. Is that about right?" Harley nodded.

"His name isn't important." She said that it might be. But Harley again said that he didn't want his name associated so that no one tried to name things for him. "Okay now?"

"Yes. Okay, you've given me the pre-information. Tell me what he has to say." Selma told her about the man and his treasures and where they were. Before she could change her mind, the three of them went looking for one of them in the basement. She found it before Ayden got home and was looking for the second one after dinner. They were making it a family project.

The first one was nothing more than a leather bag full of silverware. It was beautifully decorated, and he had asked that they sell it for something for the charity. By the time they were able to find a few more items, Ayden had said that they'd have to make sure that no one claimed the money from it. That is just what the man didn't want to happen.

"He's related to Donnie." Oh well, that made things different. She could understand now why he didn't want anyone to know. After doing a little digging, the man who had lived here when the first part of the house was built had been the great too many to count grandfather of Donnie, and he was almost as bad as his grandson back when he'd been alive. That was why he wanted to make amends. Because he'd been a bastard all his life as well.

"I don't know that we can do this without causing trouble." She didn't want things to come back and bite them in the ass, so they contacted an attorney to help them out. As it was now, they had thousands of dollars worth of silver, gold, and gems that looked to be diamonds. After consulting the man, it was discovered that he'd stolen the stuff in the house before he'd died.

"This is more and more complicated. It's stolen goods, and until we find the rightful owner, then we can't use them. You have to see where this would get us into trouble." Selma told them that he seemed like a nice man. "Of course, he does now. He's making amends, like he said. I would imagine that the apple doesn't fall far from the tree when it comes to Donnie and his distant relatives."

"I'm so sorry. He was so nice to me." Ayden asked her if any of the ghosts were mean to her, and it took Harley to get her to tell the truth. "What do you do to them when they get nasty with you?"

Her daughter had two bruises on her shoulder and one on her back from one of the ghosts. It was frightening for her to think of her child as being hurt by the dead, but Selma said she was handling it by sending them away. She told them that Harley was there to protect her, and that was when she found out that while she couldn't see the ghosts, she was intimidating enough that she could send them away when they didn't realize she wasn't supposed to be able to do that. It was in their mind that she could, and they believed her.

Putting all the things in a box in the garage, they decided that they weren't going to look for any more of them until they heard from an attorney. The things weren't bothering anyone where they were, and the man was just going to have to get over the fact that he couldn't help, for now, at least. They were doing the best they could right now in figuring things out. Even Selma seemed to be a little upset that the things were to be used to help the people being displaced.

"I wanted to help. I guess I'm not as useful as I thought we'd be." Summer asked her what she meant. "I want to be able to help the people like we were when Gilbert was around. I mean, wouldn't it have been nice to be able to start over in a new place? I know we might not have met Dad in the process, but you guys are doing so much, and me and Harley want to be a part of it."

"You can." She asked her how. "You'll need to help me with the children. I know what you guys are thinking and doing, but I don't know other kids. They might trust you more if you were to find out they needed help. You do understand that we're going to be working with children, too, to get them in a better place. We might not be able to send them away like we can the parents, but we can get them help if they're not having a good home life. And sometimes, that might even mean that they need food or some help with bills. You guys are going to be our ears and eyes on that."

"You think so?" Ayden told their daughters that he knew so. "I've been keeping an eye on this little boy at school. I mean, his parents are wolves and all, but they don't treat him right." Ayden asked what she had seen. "He's supposed to be getting hurt when he plays in the schoolyard. But he's so sore all the time. All he does is sit on the bench and wait for us to go back inside. Then he has no food for his meals either. Harley and I have been packing him things that he could put in his cubie hole, but it's not enough on account of him having a little brother at home, too."

"What's his last name?" Summer hadn't realized that Lica and Brandy would need to know this because they were in charge of the pack, and if a child was being abused, he would see to it that he was in a better position to be cared for. As soon as he had the last name, Ayden changed the subject, and she knew he was talking to his older brother. "You guys have any ideas on how we can make it so that less kids go hungry? We're trying to get more jobs for people, but it's been difficult to get things moving. Brandy had three offers of people coming to put in places to work. But with the mayor having his own crises, it's been stalled."

The four of them talked throughout dinner and clean up. They did have a cook, but tonight was his night off, and they were having dinner on the grill. It was very cold out, with it only being a few days until Christmas, but it was nice to have a nice hotdog with potato salad for dinner.

"Hello, the house." Lica showed up about the time they were having graham cracker applesauce cake for dessert. "I've just been out and about in the pack, and I was thinking that I need you girls to help me with a few projects. Not just with what you told your dad but more things like that. Are kids getting enough food at school and home? Do they have the supplies that they need to get their work done or even started? Things that would make it easier for the kids to be able to study and do better in school."

"No one has any supplies but us, and we share." Lica told them that there was money to supply supplies for the kids in the classroom. "They're not getting them then." Harley looked at her sister, and when she nodded, she looked at Lica. "The teacher we have has a new car. I heard her telling someone that she got it with the supply money because no one ever checks to see if they use it for. And she said that she has her kids in her classroom not saying anything, or she'll give them failing grades. I don't care if I get failing grades. I want them to have what Selma and I have all the time."

"What about the lunch program? Is it working?" Harley said that as far as she knew, everyone had to bring their lunches because there was nothing to cook. "Are you saying that there aren't any hot meals at the pack house?"

"There isn't even any cold food. And the milk that they give us when it's break time is warm and yucky. Selma and me, we bring in what we can, but it's not enough." He asked them why they didn't say anything earlier. "I'm not a wolf, and I didn't know that stuff was around."

"Okay, that's my problem. Thank you. I'll look into this tomorrow." Selma asked him why he wasn't looking into it tonight. "The school isn't open."

"So? That would be the best time if you asked me. There isn't going to be anyone asking you what you're doing there if they — if they know you're coming, we'll suddenly have hot food and stuff. You need to have a look around — don't you know how to be sneaky? Sheesh, Uncle Lica, even as a kid, I know that people will only let you see what they want you to see if they know that you're coming." He asked her when she'd gotten so smart. All she did was roll her eyes at him, and it made her laugh hard. "The teacher who has the new car doesn't even come in until lunchtime. Then she sits around, making us read a book until it's time to go home. There are other teachers too. Mrs. Solo teaches math, and she's only teaching us stuff like one plus one. It's so easy, but she said it's because she doesn't want to waste her time grading papers and hearing how her students are failing. Also, there is a Mr. Breman. He's...you know what? All the teachers need a good swift kick in the butt. We're only doing well in class because we were taught before coming here. It's just too boring for us, and we're not even the smartest kids in the class."

"Why didn't someone say something before?" She asked him if some kid came to him that wasn't related to him would he believe him if he said that the classes are too easy? "You might be right on that, too. Maybe I should have come to you guys earlier. I just heard that the classes were doing really well, and I never thought to have a look around."

"On account of you just hearing what they wanted you to hear." Lica looked at his brother and then at her. "You don't have to believe us or not, Uncle Lica, but I want you to know that I'm not going to get into college knowing every day that one plus one is two."

"No, I don't suppose you will." He laughed. "All right. I'll go over there tonight. What is it that I'm looking for? You said all the teachers, but going over there on a Sunday night, what do you want me to look for?"

They handed him a list. Like at some point, they expected him to be able to get his head out of his bottom, not her words, and get this taken care of. In addition to the teachers' names on the list, there was the breakfast program, lunch programs as well as a couple of other things that she'd not heard mentioned. They had a list of after-school projects that had been left undone, as well as some things that the school kids did for the community that hadn't been touched in over five years. Her little girls had been busy.

"The school nurse is a joke. She's not been

there since we've been there, and when one of the kids is hurt on the playground, they're told to not say anything, or they'll fail them. They have a real prison-like thing going on if you ask me." Lica laughed, but not for long. Harley took him to task. "You might think this is funny, but without good teachers and food, some of the kids are really falling behind. There is this one kid in the class, his name is Buck, the teachers stand him in the corner from the time he gets there until it's time to leave. It's because he wanted them to let him go to the library. And don't even get me started on the 'library.' There isn't a book there that is younger than me. And a lot of what mom calls smut books for the teachers. Also, there is a really expensive coffee machine in there that the teachers all use. I hate to say this, Uncle Lica, but I'm not very proud of you."

She thought that it hurt him to the core to be told that, especially from Harley. Selma agreed with her sister, but the words had come from Harley, who rarely had anything to say about anything. As he was gathering up the things that they'd given him, it was Ayden who went to the school with him. He said that he was going to ask

Harley to be his second in things like this, but he was afraid of disappointing her again.

Lica would take care of this if only to get back in the good graces of her children. He looked crestfallen that he'd failed them so much. As soon as they were out the door, Lica and Ayden, the girls asked her if he was mad at them.

"No, not at you, but he is at himself. Like you pointed out, he was lacking in getting even the basics for the school taken care of. I think you did right in talking to him." Selma asked if he'd tell on them for talking. "No, he'd never do that. He is a good man, but I think he was handed things that weren't up to par as he'd been told they were. Yes, the school is doing well, but at what cost is it taking from the kids. No, he's going to thank you for helping him soon. I'm betting that he's feeling bad about it already for not thanking you before he left."

At least, she hoped so. She would hate to have to go and tell him that he disappointed her too about her kids. She'd tell Brandy about it, and the man would have hell to pay.

Chapter 6

The school was a mess. Not only had they been slacking on teaching the kids, but it also looked like the place hadn't been cleaned in all the years that it had been there. And he was just sick about the library.

There were books on the shelves, but they were more to do with smut, as Summer called it, than anything to do with the kids. The entire preschool section had been removed and put into boxes that were so covered with dust that it made him sad. Ayden looked at the expensive coffee machine and wondered how they would justify that if asked. The entire school looked like it had been closed for years rather than just over the weekend. Then they went into the yard.

The playground equipment was rusty and had nails hanging out of some of the pieces. The swing, long since broken, and the seats looked dangerous, like something that one might find in a war zone. Not only was the equipment in ill repair, but he didn't think that the parking lot, other than the teachers' lot, looked like it had been repaved in years.

"I know that I just signed a work order for the lot to be repaired. Other than where the teachers park, it looks like they used the money for something else. There isn't any way that they used all that money for the little bit of lot that they have." Ayden asked his brother when the last time he was here. "I'm sorry to say that I don't know that I've ever made a trip here. I was getting good reports, and that's all I cared about. Out of sight, out of mind kind of thing."

"No wonder the girls wanted to talk to you about it. It really does look like no one has cared long before you took over the job of alpha. I'm betting right now that if Brandy knew about this, heads would be rolling. She'd be all kinds of pissed off about all this." He said that he was going to tell her before they left. "I think that's a good idea, but I don't want her coming down on me about it. I don't work here."

The two of them laughed, and Ayden told him to give him a heads-up about telling her.

When his brother told him that he was talking to her now, he decided that he was ever so glad that his daughters had been the ones to mention it rather than him. Hell was going to be paid, and he was thrilled that he wasn't going to have a thing to do with it.

Entering the barn that was to hold the mowers and other outdoor equipment, he was dismayed to find a single mower that looked like it might have been about fifty years old and nothing more. There wasn't even a shovel there to use to get the snow off the sidewalks. Yes, he thought a lot of people were going to lose their jobs over this.

Brandy showed up just as they were looking into the kitchen. There was equipment there, a newer microwave, and nothing but old, broken-down things like desks and chairs. Even a desk had been put in the room that only had three legs, and most of the vinyl had been pulled off to make it look like it would be better served in the trash dump. He couldn't believe that his daughters had been going here all this time, and he'd not had any idea. Brandy caught up with him when he was in the rooms that his daughters were in.

"Your daughters are going to be paid for

bringing this to our attention." He said that they would be thrilled to have it cleaned up more than anything. "I think we're going to have to start over is all I can think about. From the buildings to the teachers. I just can't stand the thought that I was excited to have my children going someplace so nice."

He pointed out the big pile of books that was still in boxes. There were boxes everywhere in the buildings, and he didn't even have a clue what they were holding. If he was honest with himself, he didn't want to know what was in them. For all he knew, it could be more items for the teachers.

"Will you be here when the teachers start showing up?" Brandy looked around and then at him as he waited for an answer. "They're going to take it out on the kids, mine, I'm thinking, since you two are here with me."

She asked him if he wanted to go home. Before he could answer, even if he knew what he was going to say, he saw the first car pull into the lot. It was one of the janitors coming in to presumably shovel off the walkways. He just then remembered that he'd not seen any salt around.

"He'll be able to call school. I didn't think

that he was the one to do that, but I'm guessing since he's out there with a ruler measuring the depth, that's his job." He, too, was driving a brand-new truck. He'd bet anything that it wasn't any more than a few months old. "Brandy, he's leaving if you wanted to talk to him."

"I don't. Not yet. We should be getting the call here in a few minutes that the school is closed. That's a good thing. It'll be easier for us to have a thorough inventory of what needs to be taken care of. And what has to go. I was serious when I said that the entire place needed to be taken to the ground and all the teachers fired. I believe, too, this is why we've had such a high turnover of teachers this last couple of years." He asked her if she thought it was because they'd been so disappointed. "Either that or run off. They have the ones in place that they have here that are going to play ball with them. All others would be run off I think. Did you notice too that there are newer buses? I believe that it's to make it look good for the parents. Like your daughter said, no one is going to believe a bunch of kids complaining about the school they go to."

They were there for another three hours.

School was canceled, but it had more to do with the weather than the things they were finding. Calling the police at eight, they also could gather up the teachers. They were all brought to the school to be 'talked' to about what they had found. The first teacher that was brought in was the one who seemed to be in charge.

"What do you care if a bunch of kids are complaining about classes. I mean, that's what kids are...how long have you been here?" Lica told Mrs. Holly Branch—even he thought it was a stupid name how long he'd been there. "Look, we have things under control, and you don't need to worry about things. I have it under control."

"You said that, but it looks to me that we're running a spa here for teachers who are getting paid to teach. None of that seems to be going on." She asked Lica if he'd gotten her reports. "Yes, but it doesn't really show the whole picture, does it?"

"Why are you bothering with all this? The kids are learning. You have a good group of teachers. You shouldn't be bothering yourself on something like this." She eyed him hard. "Those nieces of yours talked, didn't they? "I don't know why you'd care about them. You do know that they're only human, right? I mean, what do they expect? For us to cater to their every need simply because they're sort of related to you? Get real. Just tell them that I'll have a talk with them when they return tomorrow, and that will be the end of you coming around. We don't need someone sticking their noses into what we have going on here."

"They're my nieces, no matter what they are." She actually patted him on the shoulder and told him to go on believing that. "What's that supposed to mean? I do believe that they're my relatives. They're my brother's daughters."

"Whatever. Look, you just let me talk to them, and you'll have no more trouble from them. I knew they were going to be trouble in the first place. Always having their noses into—did you know that they've been bringing in food for the ones that don't have it? That's only going to cause us more trouble than we need. You nip that in the bud right now, or I'll have to. As I've said, you don't need to be worrying over something that you have no control over in the first place. We've been doing this my way for a while now, and there isn't any reason for it to change now. What are you going to do, fire us all? We both know that's not going to happen."

"It's exactly what's going to happen. You and everyone that works here—" She told him to shut up, and Ayden took a step back when he felt his brother's wolf run along his skin. When she smacked him on the face, both he and Brandy took another step back. Things were getting out of hand, and he didn't want to have to kill someone over this. But it was surely looking like that was going to happen. "Do you have any idea who I am? I'm your alpha. You'll do what you're told, or so help me, I'll take pack action against you."

"Like I'm supposed to be afraid of you. Look. You've been alpha for all of what? Eight months? I've been running this for the last ten years. You have no say over me and what I do here. None of the teachers are going to listen to either of you." The shift from man to beast was quick, and the woman smacked him again. It was over almost as soon as her hand was back at her side.

At some point, other teachers had entered the room. As the police, pack police, were handcuffing them, Holly lay on the floor between them, bleeding out. Ripping her throat out had been all on Brandy. When Holly had hit Lica for the second time, she didn't even shift but morphed her hand into a great claw and tore her throat completely out, beheading her in the process.

No one else had anything to say as they were being cuffed and put into a room to be fired. Lica didn't say another word, and neither did Brandy. But if the anger rolling off of the two of them was any indication, the remaining teachers would be lucky if they lived to the end of the day.

By six o'clock that evening, the school was slated to be torn to the ground. Nothing would be saved, not even the nice coffee machine that was in the place. All the desks, chalkboards, and anything else that had suffered from neglect from the staff was left to be taken to the ground as well. Lica had a crew starting on the new school the next morning. It would not only be a new place with much better learning, but there was going to be a great deal of new in the new place as well.

"There will be large trailers needed for teaching brought in to work out until the end of the school year. After that, they'll be used for other projects in the pack, such as housing for some of the things we have going on. It'll be watched over as well until we can get the cameras up and running." Brandy was barking orders at everyone, and no one dared to second-guess her. When someone had a question about what was going on, they were sent to him. He seemed to be in charge of the entire project, and he was all right with that. Lica and Brandy left about the time the bulldozers showed up, and he was delighted to have them starting the work even as he stood there watching.

Going home to his family at eight that night, not only was he glad to see them, but he needed hugs all the way around. It had been a productive day, but it had also been a very stressful one. There was a call out to other packs for temporary teachers as well as other staff to start in the fall when the new buildings were slated to be up and running. Telling his daughters what had happened. He'd never been as proud of his brother and sister as he was in that moment. They had made his little girls happy by not disbelieving them when they were talking about what had been happening at the school. They were more than a little thrilled, too, to know that Mrs. Branch was no longer going to be a part of the new system.

He was going over the ledgers that they'd been able to unearth about the spending. All the teachers had been getting bonuses from the money that had been coming in from the pack. It didn't matter what your job was, either. If you taught there, cleaned, or were supposed to cook, they were bringing in bonuses that paid not just for new trucks but vacations and holiday homes for everyone who worked there.

"Brandy just called. She wants to meet the girls at her house in the morning. I had to ask her what she wanted, and she promised me that they'd be just fine. I really was worried about it after what you told me happened today." He told her again how Branch had hit Lica. "Yes, so you said. I'd like to think that I'd be that protective of you, but you're more a wolf than I am. So I don't know how that would work with me saving your ass all the time."

"You'd have ripped her throat out even not being a wolf. And you know that Brandy wasn't either when she met Lica. Maybe we should try things out about you shifting. I smell wolf on you, but that could be just me and us making love all the time." They had been, too. Every time they were alone, they were naked and having sex. He loved it. "Did Brandy tell you what she wanted with the girls? I mean, she mentioned that they'd be paid for helping them out, but I don't know what that would entail."

"I think that they're a little overwhelmed about things right now. I know that Harley has been asking questions about what happens to them. I think they're a little worried, too, after talking to you about Branch. What made her think that she could just hit their alpha and get away with it." He told her what he thought. "I suppose she's been in charge for so long she didn't figure that anyone would challenge her anymore. I was thinking about her family."

"She didn't have one. I looked. No children either." Summer asked him if she was even a wolf. "Yes, she was at that. As were the other teachers. All of the staff have been arrested for misappropriation of funds. They'll all face jail time and will have to pay it all back. All the new cars and vacation homes will need to be sold off, and the money will be returned to the pack house. It'll be a lot of money *if* we can get it all back."

"You don't think that we will?" Ayden said that he didn't know, but as it had been going on for a while now, it was hard to tell. But he was going to be doing the work on the new place, the hiring as well as the other things that are going on. "It'll be hard to get teachers to come here, don't you think? After killing one of them."

"More than likely, it'll be easier. It'll show that Brandy and Lica aren't going to take any shit from people, and it'll be a safe place to work too. The teachers will be given a bonus if they stay for the first year and after that, they'll have contracts to work with. Calling the others to make sure that we have enough teachers will have them sending their best. There is no telling how far reaching the information has gone about what was going on around here."

"I was thinking that as well." She gathered up the girls and took them to the pack house. Summer was going to stay to make sure that they were all right, and Brandy was all right with that. It took them nearly four hours, a long time, he thought, to go over what had happened and assure that the girls were going to be all right now that things were taken care of. He hoped so. It would cost him his life, but he wasn't going to allow anyone to harm his family. No matter if it was his brother and his alpha bitch or not.

~*~

Guy was enjoying the girls. They did pamper him to a point, but they didn't overdo it. They were great at fetching him drinks and handing over the remote when he was in the living room, but he was ready to go home. He'd had enough of people, and now that he didn't have any more headaches, it was time for him to find himself a place to hole up and heal from being around too many people again. He really didn't care for people all that much.

While going over the houses that he had worked on, he heard his front doorbell ring. It wasn't anyone that he knew, so he opened the door quickly, hoping to scare the person away. She grinned at him, and he didn't have any idea why, but he was charmed by her.

"My name is Lily March. I know it's a stupid name but when my parent named me, they didn't ask for my opinion. Anyway, I've heard that you're looking for a new house. Or a house, I guess. I have one for sale." He asked her where she'd heard about it. "I was at the realtor when you called. I was going to put my house on the market, but if you buy it, I won't have to go through all that. It's a great house, and it's about a hundred feet from the downtown area. Not really that close, but you could walk there. Can I come in?"

"No. Give me the address, and I'll go and see it." She told him that her car was all warmed up and that she'd take him there. "Anyone ever tell you that you're pushy?"

"All the time. It doesn't bother me. I'm just wanting to sell my parent's home and go back to LA, where I live. Everyone is pushy out there. Or not. I'm not sure. Anyway, it's a great house and needs very little work. I'm willing to give you a good discount if you don't make me have to go through a realtor. Now, those are a pushy bunch of people. Anyway. It's got five bedrooms with baths. Mom and Dad did that when they started having kids, thinking that we'd not fight over the bathrooms so much. But me being the only child, it didn't work that way." She laughed. "I like to fight with them all the time."

"They're not dead then?" She told him that they were in LA, living the dream. "I have no idea what that means. But I have things to do today, and looking at houses wasn't on my list."

"I can pencil it in for you. Your brother

Edmond sent me over. Now, there is a nice guy." He asked her if she was calling him rude. "You are rude. But, like I said, I'm willing to overlook a lot of things if you buy the house. It's really nice."

"You're not going to go away, are you?" Again, she grinned at him. "All right. Let me get my coat. And so you know, I just got home from too many people, so if you feel the need to empty your head all the time, I'm not in the mood to listen to you."

"Yep, you're rude. All right. I'll only answer your questions when you have them. I'll be in my car." As she was turning to leave, she stopped suddenly and turned back. "The land surrounding the house is about fifty acres. I'm thinking that it will be perfect for you since you seem to have it against people coming to visit you. Also, you have toothpaste on your chin, so you should maybe wipe that off before someone makes fun of you. You don't seem to me to have any sense of humor."

True to her word, she never said another word that he didn't ask about on the way there. He'd seen the house, of course. It was sitting atop a large hill in the town and seemed to have a view of the entire city. As he was walking through the house, he did take note of the things that he liked and disliked. Guy was dismayed to figure out that he didn't have as many things on his dislike list as he might well have liked. But he wasn't going to tell her that. She might just be the type of person that said she told you so, and he hated that almost as much as he hated to be around people.

The house was nice. There were things about it that he'd never thought of in a place that he owned. There were built-in cabinets in every part of the place. The room that he loved the most was the dining room.

The floor-to-ceiling windows made him want it to be summer so that he could open up the large patio doors and bring the warmth into the house. It had hardwood floors and beautiful stained glass windows in the upper part of the large windows. As he was making his way from the dining room to the kitchen, he found a large room that held things like serving platters and extra plates.

"I forgot to mention that everything that is in the house is going to go with it. I know it's a lot but if you don't want it, my parents are going to ask more because they have to rid themselves of it. Also, the kitchen has been remodeled in the last year, so that's all up to date." He asked what the house heated with. "Another thing that I wasn't allowed to tell you is that the house sits on its own gas wells. All the heat and cooling in the house is free. So long as the wells don't dry up. They've been running since before my parents were born, so I don't think that's going to be an issue either."

He loved the kitchen and its breakfast nook, which was just off the main part. The walk-in freezer had him thinking that the previous owners had entertained a great deal and that they did it up well. While he was in the kitchen, Lily pointed out that there were gardens to the house as well as a fully functioning wine cellar. There were wines there that her parents left behind as well.

He'd not asked what the house was going to cost, but he also didn't see a problem with the things that they'd left behind. Most of it was kitchen things, like the things in the pantry. Serving platters and the like, chafing dishes as well as serving items. Ending up in the living room again, he finally asked her what they wanted for it.

"You're a wolf." He told her that he was and what did that have to do with anything. "Nothing to you. But there is pack land that butts up against the land here. Some of this land has rent past due that the pack owes. It's a good sum of money. You can check your records or whatever, but it's nearly a hundred grand. I wanted to tell you that so that if you buy the place, you know that the dues haven't been paid, and they might think they can still rent it. My parent didn't want to deal with it while they were moving. And the other alpha didn't want to talk to them about it either. I don't know who you might know that can get that caught up on, but my parents are hoping to get that money paid to them so that they can buy them a summer home in Florida. Like I said, it's a great deal of money."

"I'll talk to my brother if that helps. Is that why you came to me?" She told him that it was part of it but she'd told Edmond as well just the other day. "I see. Covering your ass, I guess."

"You might say that." She told him the price, which was considerably less than he'd thought it would be. Then she handed over the contract that had been with the other leader that she said that Edmond had asked for. "You can give it to your brother or not, but Edmond asked for it. Like I said, I like him."

He could well afford the house with the money that Brandy had given him. Also, any renovations that he wanted done had there been any. The house as it set was perfect for him. When he asked her how they were to do this, she suggested that they go to the bank and finish up there.

"I have power of attorney for the house and land for my parents. The house is as is, as I said, because you're going to be taking the things that they left behind. You didn't ask, but there is a large garage that stores lawnmowers and such that they were renting from the people who worked on it, as well as a pond out back that they had stocked every year. It's a lovely spot but too much for them anymore." He told her that he'd go right now. "Good. Edmond said that you weren't the type of person to second guess yourself. If you wanted the house, you'd do it now. Good for me. I can get home in a good time and only have to return when the loan goes through to sign the paperwork."

"I have the cash." She nodded as if she knew he might say that and told him that it was even better. As soon as they arrived at the bank, the paperwork was all filled out, but for his name, he was finished in an hour, and he was the new owner of a house. Not that he had that much to move, but he decided that he was going to move in as soon as tomorrow. If he could get his bed taken over. The rest of the house could sit empty for all he cared about so long as he didn't have to deal with people.

Ordering a pizza to be delivered, he was going to celebrate having a home. He'd have to tell the others sooner or later, but for now, he was going to bask in the quiet. Telling Lica that he had the contract that hadn't been covered brought up questions, but since he wasn't in the mood to answer them, he didn't. At midnight, after packing up his few things, he made his way to bed and decided that he was going to sleep in. Which to him, meant that he would be getting up at six instead of around five. He might not like people all that much, but he knew they were necessary to run a business. And since he worked for Lica and Brandy, he knew too that if he worked or not, he'd still get paid. They took care of family.

Chapter 7

"What did you want to get your brothers for Christmas? It's in a few days, and I've not seen you shop for them." He said he got it back in August for them. "Really? What did you get them? I'll wrap it up for you to put under the tree."

"We never wrap them." Ayden was sitting at the table when she'd asked him about the gifts, and the girls were with him. "We wait until Christmas week, then when we see each other, we give them to each other. It's all right."

"What did you get him?" He told her. "Socks. Which brother did you get socks for? And so you know, we're going to wrap everything and put it under the tree this year. We have a family."

"I got them all socks. Can I have some more of those eggs? They're really good." She got up to make him another four eggs, asking him why he would get his brothers all socks for Christmas. "We get each other socks for Christmas. And we get them in August because that's when the back-to-school prices are the best. We get a bag of socks and one pair of black ones for funerals, and being turned down at the bank for each of us. It's practical, and since we need them, we have them for the entire year. See? It's a good gift."

She just stared at him. Then he explained how the banker used to simply turn them down for any kind of loan, so they called them their funeral and turn down at the bank socks. He said they would make them look more professional if they wore the black ones in.

"So each of you would buy each other a bag of socks for Christmas, you'd not wrap them up, and you'd just—I'm supposing that you didn't have a tree either." He told her that the one in their living room was the first tree he'd ever had in all his life. That made her sad. "You have money now. You can buy each of them whatever you want."

He looked at her, confused, and she wanted to hug him. He didn't get it. It was something that he'd been doing all his life, and it didn't stop just because he had money and a good job now. She was going to go out that day, buy each of the men in her life gifts, and put on the tag that said it was from her and Ayden. Her heart broke each time she looked at the bags of socks not wrapped under the tree. She decided to call Brandy and Mac.

After telling them what she'd discovered, Brandy said she'd not asked Lica what he'd gotten his brothers. When he told her that he'd done it, she assumed that he'd done something special and didn't want her to know about it. Mac had said the same thing. After looking around, they both found the five bags of socks for each brother and the five pairs of socks in the same black color. None of them knew what to do.

"Did you know that this is their first tree ever? Ayden told me that this morning." She was an emotional wreck, thinking that these men who were so generous with not just their time but their hearts had never celebrated the holidays like... "That's why they were so confused at Thanksgiving. They didn't understand that families got together and had a large meal, then sat around being full. It was the first time that they'd had that kind of family over."

"Lica said that he understood that people ate big on that day, but he'd never participated. I just didn't understand that it was because he didn't know how not that he didn't want to. Oh my god, when I think of the things that he said to me that day, about all the leftovers, how much food I was having made. I get it now." The three of them met at her house and cried all afternoon while they talked about their husbands and their brothers. The things that they missed out on and the things that they'd never experienced. "I'm going to make sure that we celebrate each and every holiday on the calendar. I don't even care if it's Taco Day. I'm going to make it special for them. When I think of all the things that they missed because…it hurts me to my core to know that they, these wonderfully wonderful men, have given so much of themselves that they never had anyone give back to them. I mean it. This is going to be the first of the best holidays that I can make for them."

"We have to do this in a way that doesn't hurt them." Mac had a point. They weren't being selfish, just uninformed. As they decided what they were going to do and how they were going to fix this, it was Mac that came up with a plan. "We buy them gifts that they never would have gotten for themselves or from anyone. Games that they can play together. New sweaters even though the other one isn't worn out yet. When I think of seeing all those socks in his drawer and why there was still a package unopened in the closet, I understand what their thinking was. They weren't being mean by buying each other socks. It was practical. It was on sale in August, so they got it then and held onto it even though they each knew what they were doing. I can see them now, handing off the bags to each other in large grocery bags because that, too, would have been practical. When I think of their parents, I want to find them and beat the shit out of them."

It took them most of the day to get things set up. They had never ordered things for the holidays three days before Christmas, and so far, it was going to work. They got them all kinds of things that they should have had as a child through their teenage years. As soon as they were finished, the three of them had an idea that they'd not have to do this for the next wife, whoever she was, they were going to set the men up so that they not only had the holiday spirit, but they would hold it year-round.

The boxes and bags began to arrive that

afternoon. It helped to have money to burn so that they could make this work. Hiring a few of the pack to help them, they put large and sometimes giant blow-ups in their yards. Christmas presents that were jokes, and some that were serious. Through it all, they laughed, wondering how their husbands were going to react to their first Christmas. It was Hattie, Lica's cook, who told them to get them ornaments that had their first Christmas for them. By the end of the day, they were so excited that they had to refrain from telling their brothers and husbands. It was going to be epic, and they couldn't wait to share.

She was able to see Ayden's face when he got home that night. He was excited about the blow-ups but more so about the gifts under the tree. She'd even been able to get her daughters involved in the planning, and they were just as excited as she was about the morning of Christmas.

"You've been so busy." She told him that she had been, just for him. "You didn't have to do that. I got all I need right here with you and the girls." But she could tell that he was curious.

"How did you like the front yard?" He said that he'd seen them from the highway, and there were so many of them. "We're going to have even more by the time the girls are moving out. I plan to make every holiday the best that we can make it. We have a lot to make up for."

"I bet. The girls said that they were only able to get a couple of things for Christmas. I'm glad that—" Selma told him that they were all for him. "Me? No, that's not right. I've had good Christmas's."

"You've had Christmas. You've never had good ones. We're going to have fun this year." She could tell that he was embarrassed, but she didn't care. She didn't want to blindside him about the holidays and have him feeling bad. Instead, she gave him a list of things that the girls were getting and asked him what else he wanted to give them. They had been getting socks as well. And the funny part was, she knew that he'd paid full price for them as they didn't have back-to-school sales in November.

By the time she was ready for bed, Summer could tell that Ayden was getting excited. He kept looking out the front of the house and to the tree. There were about two hundred gifts under the tree and most of them were for him. She couldn't wait for him to begin opening them. She also knew that they were all going to benefit from him having such a lovely holiday.

"I don't understand." She asked him what he meant as they were preparing for bed. "Why are you making this big deal for me. We have children now. It should be all about them."

"Because it's never been all about you." He asked her what she meant. "You've never, not any of you have, had a holiday where it meant something. Not even your birthdays. It was just another day for you."

"But that's all right." She told him that it wasn't all right that he deserved more than anyone. "But I'm all right with how things went for us. We're who we are simply because of the way that we grew up."

"That's bullshit." He looked taken aback, and she told him that again. "You're who you are because you're a good man. All of you are. It had nothing to do with those people that raised you. If they were here now, I'd beat them to death and not think a thing about it. You were raised by people who should never have had kids in the first place. But I'm glad they did because I was able to have the best husband and friend in the world. A good parent to the daughters we have. A good man that helps others despite being so busy with things himself that he really doesn't have time. I love you, Ayden Frazier. So much that I'm not sure that words can relay to you what my heart already knows. I was so lucky that you found me and my girls that I can't tell you how happy you've made us all."

"Oh, honey." When Ayden sobbed a little, she looked up at him. "I don't know a thing about having fun with the holidays. I know you guys, you and Mac and Brandy have been good to us in our lack of—I thought about the socks that I got my brothers. Not because I put any thought into the gift but because that was what we always did. Like I said, it was practical for us to get each other what we needed not what we thought that we would like. I wouldn't know the first thing about buying a gift for someone simply because I could."

His tears moved her in a way that nothing else could have. He was genuinely upset about not having any idea how to get a gift for someone. She had realized at some point today that he'd gotten the girls what they told him. He was not looking around for anything that would surprise them, no. It was just a thing that they had asked for, and he got it. She was sure that it was the same for her. She'd asked him for something that she'd been looking for the other morning, and she'd bet herself that it was wrapped up under the tree with her name on it. He was, for lack of a better term, uneducated about getting things that he thought would be a good gift for someone.

"I'm going to teach you how to spend money on gifts." He told her that he'd like that. "It's a bit late this year, but we'll start as soon as the new year rolls around. It's your birthday in February, and we're going to get you things that we find fun and nothing to do with socks. All right?" Ayden laughed. "Good. All right, we're going to teach you how to have the best holidays in the world."

The plan was set. As soon as they got up in the morning, they were going to start putting together a plan for the Christmas holiday. So far, they were going to spend Christmas Eve in the pack house to work on things for the pack. This wasn't something that they wanted to do, but with the things that were going on right now, they needed to get things organized before the kids went back to school in January. Then, for the rest of the day, they'd be putting together a plan for the teachers to follow.

All of them had been arrested, and the entire staff was gone. The buildings were being torn down today and tomorrow, and by Christmas day, things would be clean slated. There would be nothing in the field to show that there had ever been a mess of a school.

Then, that evening, they were to go to Lica and Brandy's home for the evening meal. It was going to be epic as well. It was being catered again since there was so much going on, and no one had time to plan it. Their daughters had made placards with names on them, and she thought that they were going to be doing that for years to come.

The day after Christmas, they were going to start hiring teachers. The other packs around had been very helpful in giving them a list of teachers that would teach in the new buildings. The trailers wouldn't be like a room, but it would be the first of many changes to the kids' school year. She didn't know how to thank her girls for what they'd done in getting things squared away. Even Lica said he was humbled by what they'd gotten done for him.

Then, from the New Year until mid-January, when the kids went back to school, they'd be scrambling to get things prepared for them so that they'd be able to learn more than one plus one equaled two. At least, she hoped so.

Summer was going to see if she could help out at the school. She knew that Mac was going to be working there as well as Brandy, but she didn't want to spend all her time at the school. First of all, she thought it would be odd for her children, and secondly, she wanted to be a stay-at-home mom so she could help with homework, not assign it. Now that she'd been able to do it, she didn't want it to change.

~*~

That night, when they went to bed, Ayden had a lot on his mind. A lot of it had to do with his beautiful mate, but there were other things as well. Like the money that he'd found in the ledger that had been at the school. Nearly seven hundred thousand dollars of found money was there for him to turn over for the new schools. He wondered what they had planned to do with the money. There was so much of it that he had a feeling that it was going toward something huge, but for the life of him, he couldn't think what it might have been. All he could center his thoughts on was that the money had been on the books for the last ten years, well before his brother had taken over the pack. He called his brother as soon as he got up.

"That's a great deal of money." He said that he knew that, but he couldn't figure out how they had had it. "I have no idea why, but I have a feeling that you do know where it came from. You do, don't you?"

"I think I do. And if I do, then it's a lot worse in this pack than I thought Lincoln said it was." Lincoln Bates had been the former alpha when Lica had taken over. "I think that he's been funneling money to the teachers to keep them quiet. And in doing so, he allowed them to do what they wanted so that there would be good reports about the school so that it would get more money from the state. That's the only thing that I can think has happened."

"So he gave them free reign and money to make sure that the money that he wanted was there all the time. I wonder why it's still there? I mean, why didn't he take it with him when he left?" Lica told him what he thought. "He was waiting until the end of the year bonuses and going to take the rest? I guess I can see that. He'd have to be aware of what was going on, don't you think? There isn't any way that the entire school could run like it did without him knowing."

"I didn't know." Ayden told him that he thought he'd have gotten around to it eventually. "That's not making me feel better. I know that the girls told us what was going on, but I'd like to think that I did what was necessary to make things right. But I have to admit, I do feel like I went a little overboard with this."

"Why?" He told him that they had no buildings to teach in. "Yes, we do. They're coming soon. And there wasn't anything left for the kids in those buildings. Even the heat wasn't up to par. Had you waited until summer to react, Lica, then the kids would have thought, just what the girls did when we bought our house. That it would be put off and off because you can say things that you want to do but that doesn't mean that you're going to actually do them. You did what needed to be done, so show that you're not one to put things off. You did just what anyone would have...no, you did what you needed to do so that the people of the pack know that you're a good man and a better leader. Had you put it off, do you think that it would have made as big an impact as it did? I don't. The pack respects you for what you did, and I can't tell you how proud I am of you."

"Thank you." Ayden asked him what he wanted to do about the money. "I don't know. I'm hoping you have a plan. I can just take it and use it for the schools like it should have been done, but I have a feeling that you have a better idea."

"I've been learning a great deal about the holidays and the way that we used to celebrate it. I think that we should take the money that is found and divide it up between the families of the pack. Give each household a percentage of the money according to how many children they have in the household. We don't have a large pack, but I was figuring that a family of four would get about ten grand. That's a chunk of money for them anyway. The families with more would, of course, get more, and those that have less would get a great deal, but not like the families with kids would get. Even the elderly would get about three grand a household."

"You've figured it out." He told him how much of the money would be used to give to all the families. "that would help a lot of families this year."

"I have it worked out so that I can have the checks made out by tomorrow. I know it's a little late, but it could also help the town out with after-Christmas sales." He asked if he had to do anything. "Yes, you need to sign the checks, you and Brandy. I'm calling it the school fund. That way, we can let them know that things are going to start to improve."

Lica said that he'd meet him at the house. Having the computer print out the checks, he was about as excited as he'd ever been about this. A few days ago, he would have put the money aside for a rainy day. But after talking to his wife and children, he was excited to be able to do this for the other families. However, he didn't know how his brother would feel about him getting a check as well, but in order to make it fair, it was what they had to do. Everyone in the pack would receive a check.

His would be a little more because he had two children, but his brothers would get about fifteen hundred dollars apiece. Then, the married ones would be about twenty-five hundred. He met both he and Brandy there ten minutes later.

"I'm going to hire you to work on the ledgers from now on." He told Brandy that he didn't know that he'd be able to find money all the time. "It doesn't matter. You did great with this, and the pack is going to be grateful. I know that I will be."

Even after explaining how they'd get a check, too, they seemed to be all right with it. After putting them in the envelopes that he had printed as well, he was ready to go take them to the post office. However, they did it better by just going to each house and handing it over. They got to see the gratefulness on each face as they realized that the money was theirs with no strings attached. Also, it got Lica out to see the houses that were in his pack. He was going to be making improvements on those as well when the spring and summer rolled around.

By dinner time, they had handed out all the checks. It was as if Christmas had come early for him, seeing the faces of the people they were able to help. Of course, there were a lot of people going to complain about others getting more than them, but he was all right with that as well. Next time he'd tell them, he'd think twice about handing over money that was found.

Tonight, they were having dinner with the family. He was so excited about that, having a new outlook on things that he was cheerful, even when his brothers were complaining about the money being spent. But they did perk up when Lica handed them over the checks, and it was Guy who said he was going to buy himself something special with the money and not use it to pay off something. That's what they were hoping: that the money would be something to stimulate the economy a bit, too.

By the time they were finished with dinner, he was exhausted. Having been up most of the night and early this morning getting things ready for the money, he hadn't slept all that well. Now, all he wanted to do was sleep for a few months and get up when spring was here. He didn't care all that much for the cold weather, but his wolf loved it.

He and his brothers were going to start meeting once a week to go running. They used to have dinner in town, the six of them, but things had started getting in the way. He was also going to make sure that they did that again as well. He was going to make sure that family, no matter how large or small, came first. And he was going to make sure that he lived every day like it was his last. Just as he was getting into the bed, he saw that there was a message on his cell phone.

"I got this message on my machine just now and wanted to share it with you." It was his brother Lica. "It's from Mrs. Rodney. She's raising her son's five kids, and I'm so happy that you took that into account when you were putting the money together."

"Alpha, this money couldn't have come at a better time. I had no idea how much it costs now to have so many young ones around. I've been fretting and wondering how I was going to clothe the lot of them for summer after getting them a little something for Santa Claus. Now, thanks to you and your family, not only can I get them some nice things to wear but a little something extra too. Even shoes are going to be gotten for the little ones at the same time. Thank you so much. You have no idea how much this means to my growing family."

He cried for twenty minutes. He wished then that he'd been able to help them more, but he did make a list of names for the other projects that he was taking care of. Families that were helping out, like Mrs. Rodney, were with her son's family so that they could find jobs. He was going to make sure that when times were tough all around, he was able to go and get them extras that they might need.

"You're going to hold onto Christmas year round, aren't you, Dad?" He told Harley that he had a real eye-opener. "I'm glad. I have to tell you, when Mom told me that you got your brothers' socks for Christmas every year, that I had to point out to her that she did the same thing. Selma and I got them and pajamas every year, too."

They both laughed. "I didn't even have a tree until this year." She said she knew that and sat on his lap. "What's up, little one? You seem to need to tell me something. You know that I'm here for you."

"Always." She fussed around with the hole in his shirt, and he decided that he didn't need to wear clothing until it was nothing, not even good for the rags pile. "Selma is special, but I'm not."

"What do you mean?" She told him as best she could between fumbling for words. He had a feeling that, like him, she was fumbling because she was upset. "You are special to me, Harley. You protect your sister even though you can't see what she's dealing with. Not to mention, I know you've been helping her with her chores around the house so that she can take care of the ghosts, too."

"That's just what sisters do." He told her that he knew a lot of families that didn't help one another like she did her sister. "She'd do the same for me. In fact, when I have something that I need to get done, she helps me with chores, too."

"That is what family does. But honey, not all families are like that. In fact, I was just thinking about this family I knew the other day and how none of them appreciated one another at all. Especially not their mother." He thought about the family again before continuing. "The kids decided that they were going to not work because they had their mother to do things for them. And she did it all. Laundry and cleaning their rooms. Even making their beds. But the kids, there were four of them, decided that if she was going to do it, they were going to let her have more work. Then she got sick. Still working at the jobs around the house, the kids took more and more advantage of her. I'm not telling this very good. Basically, they abused her so badly that she died young, and they didn't know what to do after she was gone. And they blamed it all on her. I don't remember all the details, but when she died, they had to sell the house and cars because…you know what, that was a dumb story. Let me tell you another one."

"Never mind, I get it." She looked at him. You were trying to make it up, weren't you, so that you'd know how much you appreciate me."

"Something like that. I've never had a story told to me before, so I guess I'm a little rusty at it." She said he'd have to get better if he was going to tell stories to their little brother. "You know you might get another sister out of the deal. What will you do then?"

"Love her like she's Selma and hope for a boy the next time. You have to keep trying, Dad. I need a little brother to protect." After she went to bed, he sat there and thought of the fact that she wanted a brother. He thought that if he had all girls, he'd be thrilled. Being one of six boys had taught him nothing about little girls. But he did like their mother, so that was good.

Going up to bed, his ass dragging, he decided that he'd have to get up early tomorrow because it was Christmas. And for the first time in all his life, Ayden was looking forward to the day more than he had forever.

Chapter 8

Waking in the middle of the night, Summer made her way to the bathroom. She'd been getting up more through the night and thought that it had to do with her being home more and drinking a lot more tea. She didn't know, but this getting up in the cold of the night was for the birds. She thought that right up until she got back in the warm bed with Ayden, he was just the right temperature for her to get right back to sleep.

He asked her if she was all right, and a sudden thought occurred to her. She wanted him. Not in the morning or a quickie during the day, but right now. Smiling at him, she was thrilled when he smiled back.

"I would like to ride you now." She moved up his body, narrowly missing his balls before she settled over him once. When she wrapped her fingers around him again and slowly lowered herself over him, he didn't move. Didn't so much as breathe it felt like to her. Afraid that she'd hurt him if she moved too fast, she rode her hips over his groin and moaned each time that he surged upwards. "This is the best way to have sex. In the middle of the night with only us two hearing us."

His shirt came open, and she pulled it free the rest of the way. Just since the girls were around had he started wearing jammies to bed. She had, too, always keeping her robe close at hand in the event that one of them needed her in the middle of the night.

However, her body moved in jerky movements at first, so Ayden wrapped his hands around her waist and showed her how to move so that they both enjoyed it. He was also nibbling on her breast through her gown, and Summer was enjoying that very much.

She was an incredibly fast learner, and soon, she was hanging on so that when he came and, there was no question that he wouldn't, but when he did, she didn't want to shatter into a million pieces without something to hold onto. Ayden was the best sex she'd ever had, and she couldn't wait to do more exploring sex with him.

"I'm coming." Her shout of release caught

her by surprise, and when she stiffened over him, throwing back her head, she knew that he watched her orgasm take her. He was the most beautiful thing she'd ever seen, and she couldn't wait for him to join her. When she collapsed over him, he lifted her head by her hair and looked at her dark eyes.

"I'm not nearly finished with you." She grinned at him. "I would love to take you against the wall and take you there, but I need to finish what you teased me to. This was entirely too quick for me to enjoy all that much. I want epic, and you cheated me."

"I would love that very much. Next time, I'll make sure that I last a bit longer." Before she could say anything more, he rolled her to her back and settled between her legs. "My, but you are very fast."

"Nope. Not with this. I'm going to go as slow as I can, but I'm telling you right now, I want to pound you until you can't walk." She loved that idea and told him as much. "Good. Both of us might be walking funny tomorrow, and I don't care who notices it.

She hummed her approval. "That sounds

very nice. What do I need to do for a good pounding? Or do I need to be really bad for you? I can do that too, you know."

Summer stopped moving. Not because she wanted to, but suddenly there was no blood in any other part of her body but her pussy. She'd heard that men would think that. That there wasn't any blood in their body but their cocks, but right now, she was sure that she'd pass out if she were to move around much more than to have him inside of her. She could see him now, her down on her knees and him behind her. She rolled around so that he was right here at her ass and ready for him to do it to her. Do whatever he wanted right then and there.

"On your knees and lower your head to the floor." The urgency was evident in her speed, she thought. She was in the position she'd imagined, and her ass was right in front of him. "I'm going to fuck you like this, then I'm going to come deep in your pussy."

"Oh yes. I would like that very much." His cock was straining almost to reach her, and he fisted his cock as he moved up behind her. She could feel the thickness of his cock, almost feel the strain it was costing him to now take her right now. Backing up a bit more, she felt his balls at her pussy and nearly came then. Christ, her need was out of control right this minute.

Sliding into her heat, she felt herself tighten around him. It wasn't enough, and she needed him now. Grabbing her hips, he pulled her flush to him. Christ, she wasn't going to last long if he kept this up.

Moving in and out of her, she watched her breasts swing to and fro. Wishing he could pull one of her hard nipples into his mouth and nip at her, he leaned down and laced her fingers into his as he took her nearly to the floor.

"Ayden, please. Help me please to come. I need to have a release." He moved his hand down her body and then into her soaking curls between her legs. One touch of her clit and she screamed out his name.

She felt her milking him and try as she could, he couldn't have any more stopped from joining him than if she'd had a gun to her head. When his release came, he threw back his head and howled. Then, he lowered his head to her shoulder and bit.

He'd bitten her before, of course. Not every

time they had sex but often enough that she looked forward to it as much as having his cock deep inside of her. When his teeth sank deeper into her flesh, she screamed out his name and begged him for more. She had to hold onto her vision or pass out when he growled low against her flesh.

When he tore at her flesh, his teeth going deeper into her shoulder, she held onto the bed as he growled again and again. This time was different, she didn't know how it was different, but it was enough that she was slightly afraid of him. Then he let her go.

Falling into the bed, she lay there. When his tongue moved over the tender skin of the bites, she whimpered a bit. As soon as he pulled her into his arms, she didn't want to be held. She wanted to get as far away from him as she could. But he held her tightly as he made sure she was all right.

"What did you do?" he said that he was sure that he was changing her. "Into a wolf? Are you sure?"

"I'm not, but my wolf wanted to hurt you badly enough that you would need to be changed. I'm so sorry, love. I didn't know that I was going to do that." She thought of all the implications that meant. She'd be a wolf. "Are you all right?"

"I am. Better than all right. Are you all right too?" he said that he was sorry that he'd hurt her. "I'm all right. I swear. But I'm bleeding." He picked her up in his arms and held her, taking her to the bathroom. She could see that the wound was already healed up. Washing off all the blood, she was back in bed with him in twenty minutes. After getting warmed up, she fell into a deep sleep and felt better than she had in years.

By the next morning, she was feeling great. Her body seemed to hum with good health and her mind was clearer than it had before meeting Ayden. She didn't worry about anything. Her mind was clicking off things like it was a well-oiled machine. After getting another shower, this time washing her hair twice, she was in the kitchen with her family and enjoying the day. Christmas had never been so wonderful to her.

By the time all the gifts were opened, Ayden having gotten her a beautiful emerald bracelet and ring, she was ready to see what the other family members had to say about this new her. As soon as she walked into the house, Lica smiled at her.

"Welcome to the pack, Summer. You're a

wolf." She wanted to giggle but acted like she'd known it all along. The others noticed it as well, telling her how much they were happy for her and Ayden. The girls wanted to know how they were to become one as well, and sadly, Lica told them that they'd have to wait until they were older. Or met their own wolf. She hadn't given any thought to her daughters being mates to wolves but was thrilled to no end that they might have the same love life that she did.

After everyone opened their gifts that were special for the day, they sat around feeling full and enjoying watching the big screen television. As they were all snacking around on desserts, she took a look at Brandy. She looked like she was in pain, and it occurred to her that the woman might well be in labor. It took twenty minutes to get her convinced that she needed to get to the hospital and then ten minutes more before she was giving birth. It was all that quick.

Baby boy Frazier weighed in at just over eleven pounds. He was nineteen inches long and had coal-black hair like his father. The streak of white running through the front was a clear sign that he was going to be the next alpha. He looked so much like his father that no one was surprised that he was named Lica Edward Fraizer. He'd go by Eddy.

~*~

There wasn't a sound in the house as he made his way to the bedroom. Guy didn't want to be at home but spend more time watching over his new nephew, but the hospital was telling them all that they needed to get home. He thought it was because they'd been carrying the little man around and showing him off to everyone. Who wouldn't on their first of many children born into the family?

"What are you doing?" He nearly shifted to his wolf when he heard someone speaking behind him. "Did you hear me? I asked you what you were doing?"

"Going to bed." He didn't move when he looked in the direction of the voice. "How did you get into my house?"

"This is my house. Now that the others are gone, I can finally come out of hiding." He looked harder at the woman standing there. "What are you staring at? I have shit that needs to be done, and you're not helping me by staring at me."

"You're dead." She just clicked her teeth at

him. "I mean, you're really dead, and you're in my house."

"Of course I'm dead. I've seen you around. You've been moving your things in since the others moved out." He asked her if the others had seen her. "No. They were too wrapped up in their own lives to notice someone like me about. Why can you see me anyway?"

"I have no idea." He made his way to the kitchen then, thinking that with a ghost in the house, a female one, he needed to be more careful of the things that he'd been doing. "I was hit in the head a few weeks ago. Could that be it? I don't particularly care for people, and I doubly don't care for dead ones."

"I'm not human. Or at least I wasn't. I was a tiger. I was killed about ten years ago when someone broke into my home and robbed me. They still don't have any idea who did it, and I've been working with the police since then." He asked her if the police could see her. "Don't be stupid. You're the only one who can see me. Why is that?"

"I said I don't know." He put away all the things that he'd brought home in the way of leftovers. Brandy had wanted to make sure that he had enough to eat since he was living alone. He'd been living alone before, and no one had given him food to take home. Of course, it could have been because he'd not been to any of their homes long enough to get food, but that was all on him. "Why are you at this house if you were killed at your own home?"

"I liked it here. No one bothered me until you came around." He pointed out that this was his home. "For now, it is. Before you get too comfy, remember that I was here first."

"But I paid for this place." He ignored her for getting himself another piece of apple pie. Of course, she had to take objections to that as well. After he put the pie away and washed up his dish, he went to the living room, knowing that he was never going to get any sleep now. "Where do you sleep or whatever you do? For that matter, what's your name?"

"Belinda Gross. Who are you?" He told her, and she nodded. "I've heard of your family. Especially your parents. They're not all that nice, are they, or at least they weren't. I heard that your father died. Is that right?"

"Mother killed him." She seemed satisfied

with that, and he continued to watch television. "She's in prison. Why don't you go and visit her? She might be a hoot to have around. She wasn't when I was a kid."

"I saw your father once. He's gone now, good riddance. He wasn't a great ghost. I can imagine that he wasn't all that great of a dad, either. They were both bastards if you ask me." He told her that no one did, but he agreed with her. "You're not terribly nice, are you? Did someone shit in your oatmeal?"

"I don't know what you're talking about. I am what I am." He wanted her to go away, but he couldn't make himself tell her again to leave. Like she had said, she'd been here before him. "The people that lived here, they never mentioned anyone haunting them."

"I didn't bother with them. They had enough trouble on their own. Couldn't hold a penny between them. If not for their daughter, I believe they would have had a pact together and died by suicide together. I've never seen such a couple like them. To think that I liked them when I first moved in here."

The two of them talked most of the night. It

was just coming up on four in the morning when he made his way up to his bed. Tomorrow, he was going to find himself some furniture at the stores with after-Christmas sales and see if he could find himself a good bed. Not that he minded sleeping on the floor with a sleeping bag, but it, like a lot of things that he was out of in the house was getting old.

She knew almost everyone in town. The good and the bad about them. Just because he was running out of things to say to her at one point, he asked her about the old alpha. She had a pinched look on her face, but she asked him what he wanted to know.

"We were wondering if he had any dealings with the school." Belinda told him that he'd had a lot to do with a lot of people around town. The banker, too. "I wondered about that. How the banker knew who was shifters and who wasn't."

"There was a book. I long since stole it. I have it if you want it." He asked her what was in it. "History about things going on. Who was into who's pants. I kept notes on everything. I think that's why I was killed. I was too nosey. It hasn't stopped me, but I know more now because no one can see me. Expect for you and that little girl. She's nice. Related to you?"

"My niece. And she is nice. Please don't hurt her." Belinda said that she'd not, but she had been helping her a little here and there. "There is a man that used to live in my brother's home. He's wanting to make amends about things that he'd done when he was alive. He's been telling them where the treasures were that he stole."

"I bet if you were to ask him, he didn't steal them until the people were dead. I have a stash of things, too. Little things that I've kept around in the event that I find something I want to be a part of. I just realized that you might have been part of the school being torn down. That's wonderful. That school had secrets that are better left untold." He asked her if the kids had been hurt. "Too many to count. But like I said, it's good that it's gone."

She told him too about the teachers and what they did to the kids. Steal their lunches or money. Never kept records of who paid what fees and would charge them several times when they could get by with it. There were other things, too, things that he didn't like hearing about but only reinforced his dislike of humans, or in his case, people in general.

Lying in his bed, he wondered how much of the information that he had now that his brother would need. There were wolves in his pack that were still taking advantage of his good nature that needed to be stopped.

Rolling to his side, he thought of other things that he'd learned by talking to the dead. So far, she was the only one that he could see, and he wondered none too happily what he'd do if he saw anymore. It would be just like him to have to deal with the dead and the living while living around town.

Closing his eyes, he thought of his family. They were all having such a wonderful time with the holidays that he almost wanted to join them. But Guy really didn't like being around people. Sometimes, his own family would bother him to the point where he wanted to run away. Getting up, knowing that he wasn't going to be getting any sleep, he made his way to his computer. The only real thing that he'd set up.

Opening the tab that he needed, he looked over the paperwork that he'd been doing. His latest contract with his publisher. He'd been writing books since he'd been old enough to spell, and it had gotten better as he'd gotten older. Now, he was on his ninth book, and he was excited to be able to put it to bed. Tomorrow, he was going to go over the contract again and then send it off. Having to fill one out with every book made him take notice of the way things were worded. He should have gone to college to become an attorney like his brother Devlin. Or a vet like his brother Ivan. No matter, he was making good money now, and that's all that mattered to him.

His phone was ringing at eight, just as he was ready to go to bed and try to sleep again. Picking it up, knowing that only one person had the number, he greeted Alex with a grin. He was wondering if the next book would be out on time and then asked about the contract.

"People are really eating up the crime novels that you're doing." He said that he had nearly finished the one that came out in three months. "Good that'll give us plenty of time to get the advertising down as well as the flyers made up. Also, did you remember to look over the contract from Hollywood Firms? They really want to make your books into a movie or two. The fact that Dana

Fisher is someone that you've entirely written your career based on has drawn a great deal of attention. People really want to meet you, too."

"I told you, I'm not going to do any book tours. I don't do commercials at all." Alex told him what they were called. "I'm not going to do a book signing either. I don't like people all that much."

"You hate them, and we both know it. But I'm all right with that for now, but if we have them making a movie, you might have to do a little PR work from time to time." He told him that he wasn't going to do it if that's what it would cost him. "I promise you, Guy, we'll get this worked out so that you don't have to meet your public."

Alex was the only person in the world who knew his real name when it came to his books. Not even his family knew that he had a different name than the one he had now when it came to getting out there. Just two weeks ago, he'd seen one of his books on the shelf at his brother's house, and wanted to ask him what he thought. However he didn't. Guy didn't know what he'd do if someone were to tell him they were good. Or bad, for that matter. He just wrote them and then wanted nothing to do with them. It was a good way for him to relieve stress. And he had a lot of it avoiding people.

It was noon before he got off the computer. After getting the contract read and signed, he went shopping. He had more than enough to get himself some household items. He really didn't need all that much, and then it was well after two before he had gotten any lunch and was out the door. Shopping wasn't something that he really wanted to do, but it was a necessity if he wanted to be able to sit in this living room anytime soon.

Belinda was in the kitchen when he arrived back home that evening. Having spent the day with people, he was in a foul mood. But for whatever reason, she would perk him up. Getting himself some dinner, he talked to her about the deliveries that would be coming in the next couple of days. One of them being a bedroom suite for his room.

"I got myself a big bed. I didn't care all that much for the extras that came with it, but I couldn't make the person understand that I didn't need a dresser because I didn't have that many clothes." Belinda said that she only had three outfits that she could change herself into, and they were the things that she'd had on the day that she'd died. "I'll have to remember that. To have better clothing on when I'm thinking of dying. I guess I should think about that daily."

"That's not funny." He told her he was sorry that he'd been going for a joke. Then he told her that he wasn't all that good at them. "No, you're not. Just stick to what you know, and you'll be fine. Right now, I'm making you a list of people that you need to tell your brother about. Some of them are pack, but others are taking advantage of the elders in his pack. Also, I would like for you to do me a favor and contact my children. They don't know that I'm dead."

"I'm sorry you said you were dead for ten years." She said that was right. "Then I don't know how your children wouldn't know you were dead."

"I have a stepdaughter that I need to have notified. My kids, the ingrates, are taking advantage of her too. She knows that I'm dead, just not that I left her everything. They're keeping her from getting it." He asked her how that worked. "When I was killed, I had an insurance policy that I'd taken out about six months before. She was the benefactor. They haven't told her about it, and they're not telling the attorneys that she's around. In a few months, the money will go to them if she doesn't claim it."

"I don't like people." She said that he had to do this for her as she needed her to inherit the money. "Why can't you go and bother her or something?" He thought of what he was saying. "All right, I'll help you, but I'm not going to be happy about it."

"I didn't know that you were ever happy." She laughed, and he decided that he liked it coming from her, even if she was making fun of him. After giving him all the information, he decided that there was no time like now to get it finished. If he put it off, he knew that he'd keep doing that until there wasn't any money left for her.

Finding the attorney was easy enough. But after a couple of calls, he realized that the place was shut down until after the new year. Making notes so that he'd remember, Guy realized that he was thinking of another book he could write with a murder to be solved. He'd solve Belindas and even put her daughter in it, with changing the names, of course. As soon as he sat down to start on an outline, he was ready to go. It was nearly midnight again before he was able to get up from the desk and get him something to eat.

He wrote for three solid days. It was flowing better than he'd had a book flow in a long time. Usually, he had to keep making corrections on it, going back and forth over details that he didn't care for. By the time he was finished for the night, he not only knew how the book was going to end but he had an idea who had killed Belinda too.

After talking to her about it and getting things set up, she asked him questions. He was all right to go get them answered as she wasn't like real people; he actually enjoyed spending time with her, but with her answers, he also knew who had set things up to look like she'd killed herself, too. It wasn't her kids, where he'd been going in the book, but someone else. He couldn't wait to figure it out with her and tell the police to get up off their asses and get finished with solving the murder. Christ, he really hated people more and more daily.

By the time his furniture had arrived, he had things going in the right direction to get things resolved at the pack, too. The way things were going right now, he knew that his brother was going to be having a lot more of the pack arrested than he thought he might. Not only was Lincoln still profiting from the pack, but he was also still running things from behind the wall of being retired. Not only was he in on it, but his wife and four sons were too. Things were set up the way they were now, and if something happened, it was going to fall back on his brother, and the others wouldn't even be in the spotlight. Mother fuckers had been messing with the wrong group.

It took him over an hour to talk with his brother. After giving him everything that he had, not telling him how he'd gotten it, he made notes on the questions he had. Getting with Belinda to make sure that he had the information that was needed. Lica wanted him to go with him, and that pissed him off, but he said he'd do it. Belinda said that she could go with him, but she wasn't going to be made a fool of. The only one that he could think would be made a fool was himself, as he was the one who was going to talk to people who weren't there. He asked her if she knew his niece.

"I do. Do you think that she'd help us? Be the go-between your brother and I?" He said he didn't know why not. That's what she did. "But how are you going to explain you knowing the information and she doesn't? I mean, you're going to have to come clean sooner or later."

This was working out to be more complicated than he wanted. However, he did want to help the elderly in his pack. As soon as he agreed to tell his brother what was going on, she flew into him at full speed and knocked him back. Whatever happened, he felt like he'd been hit in the head again and didn't care for it. As he was passing out, his head hurting worse than before, he knew that this was going wrap him up with having to deal with more people than he wanted.

Damn it all to hell. All he wanted to do was to be alone and write books. Why didn't people — dead or alive just leave him the fuck alone?

AWARD WINNING, BESTSELLING AUTHOR

Kathi Barton, a winner of the Pinnacle Book Achievement Award and a best-selling author on Amazon and All Romance books, lives in Nashport, Ohio, with her husband, Paul. When not creating new worlds and romance, Kathi and her husband enjoy camping and going to auctions. She can also be seen at county fairs with her husband, an artist and potter.

Her muse, a cross between Jimmy Stewart and Hugh Jackman, brings her stories to life for her readers in a way that has them coming back time and again for more. Her favorite genre is paranormal romance, with a great deal of spice. You can visit Kathi online and drop her an email if you'd like. She loves hearing from her fans. aaronskiss@gmail.com.

Follow Kathi on her blog: http://kathisbartonauthor.blogspot.com/